MAX MARS

THE ORION CONSPIRACY

TRIPP ELLIS

1

The first time Max Mars died really sucked. She tried to avoid it whenever possible. Though, it was getting to be a difficult proposition—she had enemies all throughout the galaxy. Trouble had a way of finding her. She was like a magnet for it.

Max was just minding her own business when they came for her. She should have never stepped off the transport. She was at a bar on Orion Station—*Plasmatronics*. Max had just ordered her favorite cocktail—Bulvacci Special Reserve Antarian Whiskey.

It wasn't cheap, and the Special Reserve was hard-to-find. It was aged 28 years in oak barrels, unlike the cheap synthetic whiskey, which was just a mix of alcohol and flavorings. It was smooth and creamy, and had a little sweetness to it. It didn't burn at all. It tasted like pie. *Life is too short to drink cheap liquor*, Max was fond of saying.

She wasn't even supposed to be here today.

The transport had been diverted and delayed due to maintenance issues. The flight crew was estimating several hours to make repairs. Max could sit on board in the stuffy passenger compartment, or get off and have a drink. The screaming baby aboard the transport encouraged her to grab a cocktail.

Plasmatronics was typical of space station bars inside transport terminals. There was a wide mix of people and aliens from all across the galaxy. The drinks were watered-down and overpriced. And the food was passable. That was another reason to order top shelf liquor—you could easily tell if it had been adulterated.

Plasmatronics had a pretty good crowd. There was always a constant ebb and flow of people in and out. There was no day or night. The place ran 24 hours a day, seven days a week—just like Vegas. Trying to maintain some type of normal sleep schedule during intergalactic travel was a nightmare. Max tried to keep her body attuned to *Galactic Meantime*, but that wasn't always practical.

An entertainment bot ambled up to Max. "Would you like to make a music selection?"

"How much?"

"3 songs for 15 credits."

"Galactic robbery!"

"I could offer you a special price of 5 songs for 15? Or 10 songs for 20?" the robot countered.

"Quite the salesman, aren't you?"

"I have been programmed with advanced negotiation algorithms to optimize both revenue and customer satisfaction."

"What kind of selection do you have?"

"I have everything. What would you like to listen to? Classical, smooth jazz, rock 'n' roll…"

Max chuckled. "This isn't a smooth jazz kind of place."

"Agreed."

"Classic rock. How about something by *Led Starship*? *Black Nebula*? *Artificial Idiots*? Surprise me."

"As you wish."

Max paid the robot, and *Helion Man* filled the bar, emanating the state of the art tetra-phonic sound system. Max sipped her liquor and enjoyed the tunes. It was much better than the shrill tones of the screaming baby on the transport ship. She was almost enjoying the moment until…

"If you could have dinner with anyone in history, living or dead, who would you pick?" a man in a suit asked as he slithered up next to Max at the bar.

"Not you," Max said, dryly. Her deadly glare should have been a clear warning to step away.

"Ouch! Crash and burn," he said, pantomiming a stinging sensation.

Enjoying a quiet drink alone at a bar was a bit of a challenge for Max, even under normal circumstances. It didn't matter where she was, it wouldn't be long before some douchebag would worm his way up to her and make unwanted advances. Max's crystal blue eyes, sculpted cheekbones, porcelain skin, and plush lips turned heads wherever she went. She was the kind of woman that took your breath away. She was fit, athletic, and had all the right parts in all the right places. She made men's IQs drop whenever she walked into a room. For the most part, they became drooling fools. With raven black hair and model good looks, she was quite the heartbreaker.

The liquor on the man's breath wafted in Max's

direction. She could see the indentation on his finger where his wedding ring was only moments before he sauntered up. If she had a nickel for every married businessman that hit on her in a space station bar, she'd have a zillion credits by now.

"Bartender, another round for the lady. And I'll have whatever she's having. The name's Tim, by the way." He held out his hand.

Max looked him up and down, ignoring his attempt to shake hands. He seemed relatively harmless. Probably an insurance salesman, if she had to guess.

The bartender slid two fresh glasses across the bar. She was young, had sandy brown hair pulled back in a ponytail, and wore a low-cut tight tank top that inspired generous tips. "That will be 134 credits."

The man's eyes bulged at the amount.

An almost imperceptible smirk curled up on Max's full lips. "Shouldn't offer to buy strange women drinks."

The man fumbled for his wallet and paid the tab. "Well, are you going to at least answer my question?"

"I already did." Max finished her drink, and started on the new one.

"Now, you and I both know that wasn't much of an answer."

Max pondered this for a moment. "Your wife. I'm sure it would make for an interesting conversation."

He tried to force a smile, caught red-handed. "Good answer. Enjoy the drink," he said, then sheepishly slinked away.

Max could eat guys like this for breakfast, but the station police weren't going to be so easy to deflect. There were two at the front door. Two more spilled in from the kitchen. They weren't screwing around, either. They moved with tactical precision, entering the bar with plasma rifles in the firing position. They scanned the compartment and advanced at a rapid pace. Max could tell they were former military. Lean, solid muscle, and no-nonsense. Well-trained for station police.

At first, she didn't think much of them. Probably looking to nab some perp, or intergalactic felon. It wasn't uncommon for cops to take down a traveler on the run. But Max knew she was in trouble when all four of them glanced in her direction, then signaled to one another.

She couldn't, for the life of her, imagine what the problem could be. She hadn't done anything illegal. She hadn't killed anyone. At least, not on Orion Station. Not yet, anyway. Unless drinking Antarian whiskey was against station regulations, she should be in the clear. She didn't have any outstanding warrants or space violations.

But the station cops were there for her. There was no doubt about it.

"Fuckballs," she muttered to herself.

Max had already planned her escape route. She did it the moment she walked into the bar. It was an old habit. She knew exactly where the exits were, and where she was going if bullets started flying. It didn't matter how far away from the war she found herself, she was never going to let her guard down. Not even a couple of cocktails could slow her response time.

Max had a decision to make. She could go for her pistol and shoot her way out. Maybe take a hostage. Or she could play it cool and just find out what they wanted.

Despite the fact that there were four of them, Max was relatively confident she could extricate herself from the situation, if push came to shove. She had been in tighter situations before.

Max continued to sip her drink. Soon, the angry barrels of plasma rifles were inches from her head. The area had cleared around her. Bar patrons parted like the Red Sea.

"Set the drink down and put your hands in the air," one of the officers said. "Nice and slow."

Max paused for a moment. She'd be damned if she was going to let the whiskey go to waste. She gulped it down and clinked the empty glass against the bar. Then she slowly raised her hands in the air.

"Mind telling me what this is all about?"

"I'll ask the questions. Stand up and step away from the bar."

Max's face tensed, but she complied.

She felt an officer behind her grab her wrist and wrench it behind her back. The cold steel of a restraint slapped against her skin, hammering the bone. The officer grabbed her other wrist and yanked it with enough force to dislocate the average person's shoulder. He twisted her wrist behind her back and slapped on the other restraint. Then he proceeded to pat Max down. The officer ran his hands along Max's thighs. She wore a skintight bodysuit that left nothing to the imagination, and the officer's fat hands slid up her smooth legs to her crotch.

Max's ass was a work of art, and this jerk had a handful of it. She clenched her jaw. If she had her hands free, the guy would probably be dead. You had to be someone special to reach Max's holy land, and this cop was far from someone special.

"You having fun there, big guy?" she asked.

"Just doing my job, ma'am," the officer stammered.

"Grab my ass again and you're gonna draw back a stump." Max glanced his nameplate—it read *G. O'Reilly*.

"Are you threatening an officer?" O'Reilly said.

"Do you feel threatened?" she said, baby talking him.

The other officers chuckled.

O'Reilly continued to frisk her and found her plasma pistol. "This is an illegal weapon."

"I've got a permit for that."

O'Reilly smelled the barrel, checking to see if it had been fired recently. He didn't indicate one way or the other if he smelled anything. Then he recited Max's rights in a dry monotone voice. "You have the right to remain silent, anything you say can and will be…" He rambled on the standard disclaimer.

"You mind telling me what you're arresting me for?" Max asked.

"As if you don't know."

"I think there's been some type of misunderstanding. I'm on my way to—"

"I don't care where you're headed. You're going to be doing an extended stay in our hospitality suite." O'Reilly barked at the other officers. "Take her away."

2

Max racked her brain, trying to figure out what she was being arrested for. The officers marched her through the corridors of Orion Station, toward the prison processing area. The hallways were bustling with activity. The massive facility had the population of a large city. There were residential sections, business districts, commercial areas, medical centers, and industrial facilities. There were even several parks with domed roofs that gave stunning views of the cosmos. Living on the station was almost indistinguishable from living in any modern terrestrial city. But the higher transient population gave the station a slightly elevated crime rate. The OPD dealt with everything from petty theft to drug trafficking, prostitution, assault, and murder.

Max was ushered through a maze of passageways to the police station. It was a state-of-the-art facility, with all the latest criminal justice technology. Like any police station, it was alive with activity—detectives working cases, beat cops bringing in detainees, and civilians filing complaints. There were giant screens tracking criminal activity on the station, as well as a predictive modeling algorithm to determine areas of potential crime. For the most part, it was accurate in determining criminal hotspots. But the random crime-of-passion was much harder to spot.

The officers pushed Max into the prisoner processing center. There was a line of detainees ahead of her. The woman in front of her was not pleased to be in custody, and was quite vocal about it. She was an orange creature with dark spots and a humanoid body. She was most likely from Tralfur. "This right here is some bullshit. I want my attorney. I ain't telling you mother fuckers a goddamn thing."

"Calm down, ma'am," an officer said. "You'll get your chance to speak with an attorney."

"How am I supposed to be calm when you've got me in handcuffs?"

"If you don't like the handcuffs, maybe you shouldn't have broken the law."

"I told you, I didn't do shit. You've got the wrong person."

The officer rolled his eyes.

She was quiet a moment, then, "I gotta pee."

The officer's eyes narrowed at her. "Hold it."

"I said, I need to use the restroom."

"And I said to hold it."

"I'll go right here,"she threatened.

"Go ahead. You won't be getting a fresh change of clothes anytime soon."

She scowled at him, but thought better of soiling herself and having to wallow in it for the next several days.

The officer grabbed her arm and pushed her along.

"Get your hands off of me. You've got no right to touch me."

The officer unholstered his STN-60 stun pistol. "One more word out of you, and you're going to take a long nap."

"Oh, no, you can't do that. I know my rights—"

The woman had barely finished speaking when the officer shot her with the neural disruptor. Her body went limp and flopped to the deck. She would be out for at least an hour, maybe two. And when she woke up, she might not even remember how she got here.

The neural disruptors were an effective, non-lethal means of crowd control. Though they weren't without risks. The most common side effects were short-term memory loss and temporary amnesia, along with a hell of a headache. In rare instances, some individuals experienced permanent memory loss, disruption of motor skills, and even stroke. The officer dragged the woman's body forward to the processing desk. It didn't matter to them whether she was conscious or not, they would still scan her biomarkers and book her into the system.

It took 20 minutes for Max to reach the processing desk.

"Name and ID number?" the officer behind the desk asked. His nameplate read *A. Murphy*.

Max said nothing.

"We're going to figure out who you are eventually, might as well save everyone the time and trouble."

Max still said nothing.

"Fine, have it your way," he said in monotone. He had an expressionless look on his face. He was so sick of his job it wasn't even funny. Booking in scumbags day in and day out wasn't exactly a fulfilling career.

Officer O'Reilly un-cuffed Max. "Don't give me any trouble."

"Place your hand on the scanner pad," Officer Murphy said.

Max just stood there and stared at him blankly.

"It's not optional."

Max still didn't budge.

"Do it, or I'll do it for you," O'Reilly said. "You might have the right to remain silent, but we can legally compel you to provide biometrics and DNA data."

"I'm well aware of my rights."

O'Reilly pulled out his stun pistol and pressed the barrel against the temple of her head. The weapon was supposed to be used at a minimum distance of 2 feet. Usage at such a close distance was likely to cause brain trauma.

Max placed her hand on the biometric scanner. She didn't particularly feel like getting shot with a neural disruptor, and they were going to get the information anyway.

"Look into the retinal scanner," Murphy said.

The station's computers would take a few minutes to connect with the Federation database and pull up Max's information. In the meantime, they continued the processing ritual. She was 3D scanned to create an accurate representation of her image. Her voice was recorded and analyzed. And a DNA sample was swabbed from the inside of her cheek.

Her complete background history should have been available within a matter of minutes. But much to Officer Murphy's surprise, the database returned no results. In all of his 16 years on the job, he had never processed a suspect with no result. His face twisted up perplexed. "Who the hell are you?"

Max continued to exercise her constitutional right to silence.

"Have it your way. But I guarantee you this, we will make you talk," Murphy said.

Max took it as a challenge. A slight smirk curled on her lips. She had already been to hell and back, and she knew there wasn't a damn thing that Officer Murphy, or anyone else in the OPD, could do to her that hadn't been done before.

"Put her in Interrogation 2, and let Detective Reese know."

Officer O'Reilly marched Max down corridors and shoved her into a spartan compartment. The hatch slammed shut behind her with a solid clank. He sneered at her for a moment through the polycarbonate viewport, then left.

It was a typical interrogation room. A desk, two chairs, an overhead light, and a two-way mirror. There was smooth easy listening music playing over the loud-speakers, and Max figured they were probably pumping in subliminal messages to help aid compliance.

Max took a seat and waited for the detective. This was turning out to be a crappy day, and sitting aboard a stuffy transport with a crying baby was starting to sound like a much better way of spending the afternoon.

3

"Sign this," Detective Reese said. "It will make everyone's life easier." He slid a smart glass tablet across the table, placing it in front of Max.

Her eyes glanced to the screen and surveyed the prewritten statement. Her face tensed and her cheeks grew red. Rage boiled under the surface, but she tried to maintain her composure. It felt like the walls were closing in around her. She felt a thin mist of sweat form in the small of her back and in between her breasts. Her heartbeat elevated, and she could hear her pulse pounding in her temples. Max didn't like confined spaces, and if she signed this document she was going to be confined for a long, long time.

"Place your thumbprint in the confirmation box." Reese had a smug grin on his face. He knew he had his suspect nailed *dead to rights*. Reese was an average looking guy with brown hair and brown eyes. Mid 30s. Cheap suit. "It's an open and shut case. I've got a witness that places you at the scene. And the nature of the crime is going to lead to an exceptionally harsh punishment. Judge Abernathy doesn't look kindly on this type of thing. Take the deal. It's in your best interest."

Max glared at the statement on the tablet for a moment. Then, with her fingertip, she wrote on the screen. She spun the device around and slid it back across the table to Reese.

He tried to hold back a grin as he looked over the statement, preparing to gloat. He was a good detective, and he liked closing out cases quickly. But his grin faded when he read what Max had written. It wasn't a signature.

Fuck you.

Reese scowled at her. "So, you want to do this the hard way? Okay. We'll do it the hard way then. And I promise you, you'll regret not taking this offer." He tapped his earbud. "Calhoun, do you want to step in here for a moment?"

Reese eyed Max with his trademarked smug grin again. A few minutes later, Officer Calhoun stepped into the compartment. She was a good-looking blonde in her early 30s. She had a banging body, and the tight OPD uniform accentuated it. She glared at Max as she entered. Her blue eyes were red and puffy, like she'd been crying. She had a look of pure hatred in her eyes, and Max could tell she was just praying for a few moments alone. "Yep. That's her alright."

"Are you sure?" Reese asked.

"Positive."

"Thank you, Officer Calhoun. That will be all."

Calhoun didn't leave. She continued to glare at Max. Her hand hovered precariously close to her sidearm.

The look on her face said *fuck her career. Fuck her pension. One moment of revenge would be worth it all.* It was easy to see that this was personal for her.

"I said that will be all, Officer Calhoun."

"Yes, sir," she stammered. Calhoun backed out of the compartment and closed the hatch.

"She's lying," Max said.

"Officer Calhoun is a respected member of the force. She has an outstanding reputation. No disciplinary actions. Who do you think a jury is going to believe? Her, or you?"

Max was getting railroaded.

"And who are you, anyway? We're going to find out."

"I want to speak with my attorney."

"One will be provided for you."

"I don't want a public defender. I want my attorney. Marc Gotro on Beta Epsilon 2."

"Sorry, princess, you're getting a public defender."

"I have a constitutional right to choose my own attorney."

"Seeing how you won't tell us who you are, and I have no way of verifying who you are, or if you're even a Federation citizen, you have no rights." He flashed that smug grin again and leaned back in his chair. "As far as I'm concerned, you are an enemy combatant. You're lucky you're getting access to a public defender. Considering the nature of your crime, you're lucky you're still alive. Cops around here don't take too kindly to that sort of thing."

There was a long moment of silence.

Max contemplated her options. She wasn't hand-cuffed. She could easily lunge across the table and snap this jackass's neck. Reese had been dumb enough to carry a weapon into the interrogation room with an unrestrained prisoner. She could snatch his pistol, take out the first few officers that stormed into the compartment. But that would probably just make her situation worse. Best to just let the things unfold and see where they led.

Reese leaned in and spoke in a calming tone. "Look, the way I see it, I'm the only friend you've got around here. I'm a lot more levelheaded than some of the other guys. I'm offering you an opportunity for the best possible future. Trust me, you don't want to see this thing go to trial." He paused a moment. "You're young. If you take this deal, you'll be in minimum-security, you're out in 25 years. With the way modern medicine is, you could live to be 250, maybe 300 years old. You will still have plenty of life left. You'll be able to start over, and make something out of yourself."

Max glared at him. Fuck 25 years. That might as well have been an eternity. She probably wasn't going to live near that long.

"What's it going to be?" he asked.

4

Max didn't trust anyone, attorneys least of all. She certainly didn't trust the public defender provided by the same government that wanted to convict her of murder.

"I am legal unit 1977-1138. Thomas H. Xavier. But you can call me Tommy, if you prefer."

Max liked robots even less than she liked most people. And she found most people to be rather disappointing. She'd only met a few people in her lifetime that she could truly trust. People that had her back. People that would do anything for her. People who would sacrifice. Unfortunately, the majority of them were dead.

Tommy was made of composite materials and had a humanoid skeletal framework. Hard surface panels covered his intricate machinery and gave shape to his form. Robots, androids, and other forms of artificial intelligence were highly regulated. Though synthetic skin and bio-mechanical technology had been refined and perfected, it was illegal to produce an android that

was indistinguishable from a human. But just because
something was illegal doesn't mean people didn't do it.
The underworld was filled with humanoid pleasure
bots that were identical to humans in every way. If you
wanted to have an illicit fling with your favorite
celebrity, you could do it with an identical pleasure bot.
For the most part, law enforcement looked the other
way, with the occasional crackdown here and there. But
what they didn't want were humanoid androids
running around polite society demanding equal rights,
the ability to own property, and more importantly, the
right to vote. It wouldn't be long before the robots could
reproduce themselves in such sufficient quantity as to
vote themselves into total and complete power. Robots,
androids, and artificial intelligence existed solely to
serve to the benefit of mankind. Behavioral inhibitors
kept them from acting in their own best interests. But it
was probably only a matter of time before they were
able to circumvent the hardcoded laws of robotics.
When that happened, humanity would no longer be the
dominant intelligence in the galaxy.

"Everything I say to you is recorded, correct?" Max
asked.

"Yes. I keep detailed records. I am able to recall
conversations and events with exact detail, unlike
human attorneys. I am also able to instantly analyze
conflicting statements, and determine truthfulness
based on voice stress analysis. I have the entire history
of recorded caselaw at my disposal, and I excel at
exploring the nuances of the law for my client's benefit."

"What's to keep the prosecutor from getting access
to your data?"

"We have an attorney-client privilege. I will only

disclose data to the prosecutor in accordance with the rules of disclosure."

"And what if you get hacked?"

"That would be impossible. My encryption algorithms would take 170 years to decrypt using the entire processing power in the known Federation."

"And you expect me to trust you?"

"I could lose my certification to practice law. I would most likely be decommissioned and scrapped. Synthetic attorneys are independently monitored by the IAAIA."

"Are you any good?"

"I perform my functions with 99.997% accuracy. Judging by the evidence, the jurisdiction, the judge, and past outcomes in his court among similar cases, I was able to negotiate a deal for you which is an improvement upon the initial offer. 20 years, minimum security, eligible for parole in 15. It is my professional opinion that you take the plea agreement."

"Unacceptable. "

"You're being charged with the murder of a police officer. Under the circumstances, I think this is a very good deal."

"Not if you're innocent."

"I am more than happy to enter a not guilty plea and defend you in court. But I cannot guarantee a positive outcome. They will ask for the death penalty, and the odds suggest that they will get it. I have run an analysis of every homicide of a police officer in this jurisdiction. In every case, a guilty verdict was rendered against the defendant."

"Don't you find that a tad bit odd?"

"Are you suggesting some type of corruption or

collusion among the court system?" Tommy said it as if it were unfathomable.

Max scoffed and shook her head. "Something is rotten in Denmark."

"We are not in Denmark, and I'm not sure how that is relevant to the situation."

"Their case is a complete fabrication. I don't even know this cop."

"Officer Chase Carter."

"You don't find it strange that I'm charged with the murder of a person that I've never met and have no connection to?"

"It happens all the time. It is not for me to say why humans behave in the manner that they do. Despite my vast database, human behavior is still a mystery to me. You act in the most illogical of ways, at times."

"Look, I'm telling you, I was aboard a transport to Proxima Minor 5. I stepped off to get a drink and that's it. I never set foot out of the terminal, or into the station proper, until I was arrested. Surely you can find some security camera footage of the transport or the bar that can prove I was nowhere near the scene of the crime at the time it occurred."

"The data from the security cameras seems to be corrupted at the moment."

"Figures." Max was silent a moment. "How about you use that 99.997% accurate neural processor of yours and tell me what motive I would have for killing a cop on this station?"

"Perhaps if you would be willing to identify your-self, there may be elements in your background that could speak to your character. It might help in your defense. As it stands, you are a transient drifter without a name."

Max glared at the talking appliance. "You tell the DA he can shove this bullshit case up his ass."

"Do you want me to use that exact phrasing?"

5

A nother few seconds and Lucian was going to die. Any display of weakness in prison either resulted in death, or indentured servitude. It was a good thing Max wasn't ever one to display weakness.

Max was escorted to a temporary holding pod which would become her new home until she completed the trial and faced sentencing. If she survived that long, she'd be sent to a super-max prison somewhere. Having turned down the minimum-security plea agreement, they'd hit her with everything they had, if she was convicted.

There were several privately owned super-max slams throughout the Federation. Usually located in inhospitable environments, making escape impossible. Prisoners were often brutalized, malnourished, or sold into slavery. Once you found yourself in the correctional system, your life became meaningless. And it was damn near impossible to get out. And if you were fortunate enough to get out, a plethora of different agencies popped up requesting fines related to your offense. A simple OSCWI (operating a spacecraft while intoxicated) would run you afoul of multiple agencies. 25,000 credits to the Department of Space Vehicles. 22,000 credits to the Intergalactic Transportation Bureau. 15,000 credits to the Clean Space Initiative (interstellar space junk was becoming a serious problem). And 10,000 credits to the Galactic Space Council, which was a nonprofit organization that no one could seem to determine what their function was. For an offense like murder, the fines could range up to a million credits.

But murder was an everyday occurrence in the holding pod. For the most part, the guards didn't seem to care what the inmates did to one another. The only reason they tended to break up fights was so they didn't escalate into full-scale riots. If the inmates wanted to kill each other, that was their business. And the guards stayed out of it. And no guard was going to rush in to save a suspected cop killer. There was no doubt, Max was going to have a tough time of it.

Junk had his massive hands wrapped around Lucian's neck. The scrawny guy's eyes look like they were going to pop out of their sockets. His face was red, and the veins in his forehead bulged. Lucian was practically turning blue.

Junk was easily twice his size. He had earned the name from the female inmates who were quite enamored with the size of his package. He was carved out of solid muscle, and not somebody who's bad side you wanted to get on.

The fight, if you could call it that, was going on in the common area. Junk had Lucian flat on a table top, choking the life out of him. It was so blatantly obvious, that the guards had to do something. A tactical response team rushed into the common area in full battle gear—weapons in the firing position. They surrounded the two combatants.

"Release the inmate, now," the squad leader yelled.

With the barrels of angry plasma rifles staring him in the face, Junk didn't have much choice. He released his grip from Lucian's throat, then backed off with his hands in the air.

"Put your hands against the bulkhead. You know the drill. Move. Now!" the squad leader commanded.

Junk complied. He put his hands in the air, backed slowly to the nearest bulkhead, spun around and placed his hands against the cold steel.

Then the correction officers rushed in and hand-cuffed Junk.

Lucian gasped for breath and peeled himself from the table. He had to follow the same drill. Against the bulkhead, cuffed, questioned, then moved into segregation. Both of them would stay in solitary confinement for the next 24 hours. It was a cooling-off period, and also served as punishment. A lesson not to start shit.

Junk glared at Max. As far as he was concerned, this was her fault. If she hadn't been arrested and ushered into the holding pod, the incident would have gone unnoticed. He was going to have to spend 24 hours in solitary confinement all because of Max. And that didn't sit well with him.

Less than a minute in the pod, and Max had already made an enemy.

The guards pushed her toward her new home—cell A-34. It was a small rectangle that looked like it might be comfortable for a small guinea pig. But two inmates per cell made it overly crowded. There were two narrow bunks, and a toilet and sink in the corner.

"Welcome to your new home, dirt bag," one of the guard's said. "Meet Spoons. I'm sure you two will become intimately acquainted before long." The guard had a devious grin, knowing what Spoons was capable of. He left Max to settle into the cell with her new roommate.

Spoons was a thin, odd looking fellow, with big ears and a square head. He looked like a mix between Flovaxian and Vercan, but it was hard to tell. He had green skin and a tail that poked through his orange prison issue jumpsuit. He sat on the top bunk and blinked his eyes incessantly as he ogled Max.

"Spoons, huh?" Max said. "How'd you get that name?"

"That's all hearsay and speculation," Spoons said. "I didn't do nothing."

Max raised a curious eyebrow at him. "That seems to be a common story around here."

"You'll learn real quick, ain't nobody guilty in here."

"Right," Max said skeptically.

"We're all innocent, just like you." Spoons winked.

It wasn't worth trying to explain to him that she really *was* innocent.

"What are you charged with?"

"Murder."

Spoons looked impressed. "Really? I figured you for a hooker myself."

"Keep dreaming."

"What, did you *off* your husband?"

"I don't have a husband."

"Of course not. He's probably dead now."

Max glared at him.

"So who did you *allegedly* kill?" Spoons asked, making air-quotes around the word *allegedly*.

"A cop."

"Oh, high five," Spoons said, holding his hand in the air, waiting for Max to smack his palm.

Max didn't move. Her penetrating eyes stared the little alien down.

Spoons sheepishly lowered his hand. "Look, I can show you the ropes around here. Give you some tips. Tell you some pitfalls to avoid. Who to be nice too, and who to stay away from. If you want. Or, you can just figure it all out on your own."

Max's eyes narrowed at him. She was always leery of overly helpful people. "And what's that going to cost me?"

"Nothing," Spoons said, innocently. "Out of the goodness of my heart. From one inmate to another."

Nobody in prison did anything out of the goodness of their heart.

"I don't plan on being in here for long."

Spoons chuckled. "Let me tell you something, sweet-heart. None of us planned on being in here very long. Not even the lifers."

6

T he brown sludge on Max's tray looked like runny dog shit. It smelled as offensive as it looked. She stared at it in disgust. "What the hell is this?"

"APN," Spoons said. "All-purpose nutrition. Or as we affectionately like to call it, dog shit."

Max glanced at him, repulsed.

"It's got everything you need to maintain nutritional sustenance." He said it in a manner that almost sounded like he was defending it. "You get used to it. It's the only thing you're going to get. Breakfast, noon, and night." He shoveled a spoonful in his mouth.

Max's stomach twisted in knots. She felt queasy. There was no way she was going to eat this slop. She pushed the tray aside and glanced around the cafeteria. It was bustling with inmates. Silverware clattered against trays, and the rumble of chatter filled the air. Many eyes stole glances at Max. Not only was she a newcomer, but she was easy on the eyes. Even if she looked like a toad, she'd be the subject of desire by the rabid inmates. Fresh meat was always at a premium. The fact that she was a stunner made the lecherous stares even worse.

"Seriously, you need to eat. You need to keep your strength up in a place like this," Spoons said. For an instant, it almost sounded like genuine concern.

"Why do you care?"

"We are cellmates. We need to have each other's back in here."

"Just like you had Drabo Star's back?"

Spoons's eyes widened with surprise. "How did you hear about that?"

"A little birdie told me."

"Circumstances beyond my control."

"I heard you sharpened a spoon and slit his throat with it as he slept."

"I can neither confirm, nor deny, that." Spoons shrugged. "He crossed the wrong people. I got tapped to take care of it. If I didn't, it would've been my ass. Hypothetically speaking, of course."

"Of course."

"All I'm saying is someone like you, in a place like this... They are going to come for you. Could be today, could be tomorrow, could be in the middle of the night... who knows? But it's going to happen. You're going to need me to back you up."

Max arched an eyebrow at him. Spoons may have been a ruthless killer with kitchen utensils, but he didn't look like he could punch his way out of a paper bag.

"Just like I'm gonna need your help when somebody comes for me."

"And who's going to come for you?"

Spoons shrugged. "It's never who you expect. But I've got my share of enemies, just like anyone else."

Max took the opportunity to survey the cafeteria. There were only two prison guards and a handful of kitchen workers.

Spoons could see in her eyes what she was thinking.

"Anybody ever escape from here?"

Spoons shook his head. "Not unless you can walk through walls."

As strange as it sounded, Max knew people who could. Beings who had full control of their atomic structure and could pass through solid objects. Eudovians. Elusive little bastards. Next to impossible to destroy. Max had gotten into a few scrapes with their kind. She wasn't keen on going up against them in battle again. Unfortunately, their special gift wasn't something that you could learn. They were born with it. Max had a lot of talents, but that wasn't one of them. If she was going to get out of here, she was going to have to do it the old-fashioned way.

A GLOWING RED force-shield sealed the prisoners in their cell at lockdown. Max wasn't particularly excited about spending the evening alone in a cell with an inmate that had a history of killing people in their sleep with utensils.

Spoons took the top bunk, and Max settled for the bottom. The mattress was a thin, lumpy cushion that had maybe half an inch of padding on a good day. Max had slept on rocks that were more comfortable. The pillow looked like a dead rat and smelled about the same. It didn't have a pillowcase and was stained from years of sweat and abuse. There was no telling what had been done to the pillow on lonely nights over the years. Max didn't want to think about it.

She didn't plan on getting much sleep anyway. She needed to get some rest, but it wasn't going to be true sleep. It would be a semiconscious nap, and she would be completely aware of her surroundings. The slightest sound throughout the night would cause her eyelids to snap open, instantly alert.

Spoons was a restless sleeper. He tossed and turned, shifting positions every few minutes. He began to snore for a few minutes, and damn near swallowed his tongue, then rolled over onto his other side and quieted down. The silence would only last a few moments before he began to snort and wheeze again. Max had endured alien torture chambers that were less obnoxious then Spoons's snoring. 25 years of dealing with irritating cellmates was not in her game plan. She didn't want to spend another 25 minutes in this hellhole.

There were no clocks in the cell. Max had no way of telling time. But she figured it was somewhere around midnight when it happened. She could hear quiet footsteps outside the cell. Then the forced shield deactivated. The containment beam was supposed to remain active until morning roll call and breakfast.

Max sprang out of her rack and positioned herself in a defensive stance. She knew something was up. Prison guards would have stormed into the cell with stun batons, riot gear, and weapons if this was a midnight check. But there were no prison guards in the area. All of the other cells remained on lockdown.

Junk appeared in the entryway to her cell.

Max didn't have any doubt about what was going on. The guards must have let Junk out of solitary confinement. It was the only explanation. And she knew damn good and well that Junk didn't deactivate the force-shield to her cell on his own. The guards were helping him. Whatever was about to go down, they had sanctioned.

Junk had a devilish grin. His massive biceps flexed. His thick hands formed fists that were like bricks. He was 6'5", 300 pounds, and built like an ox.

Spoons popped one eye open, saw what was about to go down, then snapped his eyelids shut again, pretending to be asleep. So much for having his cell-mate's back. The weaselly little coward was good for nothing. Not that he would have been much assistance anyway. Junk would have snapped him in two, like a toothpick.

Max stared her aggressor down. "Things would turn out better for you if you just turned around and walked away."

Junk chuckled. "Sorry. Can't do that."

"Really? Is someone forcing you to be here?"

Junk's grin faded. "No one forces me to do anything. Haven't you figured it out yet?"

"Figured what out. This prison may belong to the warden, but this pod belongs to me. "

"If you're the toughest thing in here, then I've got nothing to worry about."

Junk stared at her in disbelief. "I'll give you one thing, you're cocky. But your mouth is writing checks your ass can't cash."

Conversation wasn't Junk's strong point, and he had exhausted his vocabulary. He lunged for her and swung

a hard right. His fist careened through the air like a
bullet train. One solid punch from Junk was enough to
put most people in a coma.

Max moved with lightning speed. She was a blur. A
phantom. She blocked the blow with her forearm and
grabbed the beast's wrist. Then jammed her palm
against his elbow, wrenching his arm around until it
popped and crackled.

Junk screamed in agony.

A swift knee to the groin doubled the meathead
over. A sharp elbow to the back of the neck flattened
Junk on the deck.

He didn't know what hit him.

Max stepped back and assumed a defensive posture.

Junk pushed himself from the deck and staggered to
his feet. He squared off to face her, looking dazed. He
was in a state of utter disbelief. He snarled at her, like a
bull ready to charge.

"Really? You want more of this?"

Junk jabbed twice, then swung another hard right.

Max bobbed and weaved, then countered. Her fist
cracked Junk across the jaw, wrenching his neck sideways. Blood splattered from his lips, speckling the bulkhead. Crimson goo oozed from his mouth as he spit a
tooth out. It pinged against the deck, bouncing into a
cranny.

Junk had never been hit that hard in his entire life.
This girl's fist was like a sledgehammer. Men twice
Max's size didn't hit half as hard.

Junk tried to shake it off, but Max could see in his
eyes he was second-guessing himself. His confidence
and swagger were long gone.

Max watched his eyes as he tried to formulate a new

plan of attack. But Junk had never been a technical fighter. He was a brawler. Most opponents went down on the first hit. Junk had never been in a fight that had lasted this long.

He charged again and swung a crushing blow.

Max blocked, sidestepped, then slammed his kidney with another devastating hit.

Junk arched around her fist as it bore into his flesh. He groaned in pain. A millisecond later, Max put her heel into the side of his knee. The sound of the medial collateral and anterior cruciate ligaments snapping filled the compartment. It sounded like someone had broken a thick stalk of celery. His knee bent sideways in a direction that knees don't normally go.

The big meathead crumpled to the deck. He would never walk without a limp again. But Max wasn't done with him. She had him in a wrist lock, and he was going to lose the ability to use his hand if he wasn't careful. She had no sympathy for him. Junk had brought this on himself.

"Who put you up to this?"

"Up to what?" Junk whimpered. Tears of pain were streaming down the big man's cheeks.

"You didn't come in here just to get your rocks off. You had help from the guards. Someone paid you to kill me. Didn't they?"

7

The shrill screech echoed throughout the prison pod as Max snapped Junk's wrist. It was a sound that would make even the most hardened inmate cringe. The once imposing menace was reduced to a whimpering blob. He had the devastated eyes of a small child that had lost his mother in a crowded space. He looked helpless and afraid. A man like Junk had made it through his whole life on his ability to dominate other men. It was his security blanket. And that blanket had been ripped away by a girl a fraction of his size. Junk would never be able to throw a hard right again without feeling the sting of his injury. It would haunt him for the rest of his life. An embarrassing reminder of his defeat. And his dominance over the pod was gone. In the span of a few minutes, his entire world had collapsed. But despite everything, he held his tongue. Junk knew the prison code well—keep your mouth shut, hold to your word, and never rat on anyone.

"Who the hell are you, lady?" Junk stammered.

"Someone who can cash all the checks her mouth writes."

Max's victory was short-lived. A strategic response team in full riot gear rushed into the cell. They weren't going to take any chances. One of the correctional officers blasted her with an STN-60.

It should have dropped Max to the deck instantly. But she was still standing. The guard's eyes widened in disbelief.

The neural disruptor dazed her momentarily. She felt drunk, and her head throbbed. It was like she had been out all night drinking tequila. She shrugged it off and refocused herself on the response team. One of the goons was advancing with a baton. It had prongs on the end of it and would send more volts through Max's body than she cared to experience.

The officer lunged for her and clicked the trigger. The wand crackled and sparked with energy as it stabbed towards Max's abdomen.

She sidestepped and grabbed the baton. With expert precision, she stripped it from the guard and jabbed the prongs into his belly. She squeezed the trigger and zapped the bastard. His body twitched and contorted, then flopped to the deck.

Two other guards rushed in and attempted to tackle her. But she knocked both of them on their asses. They were finding out that there was something special about Max. She was no ordinary female.

Sergeant Kerns drew a plasma pistol, and aimed it at Max's head. "I suggest you settle down and comply, or I'm going to vaporize that pretty little face of yours. And I think that would be a shame, now wouldn't it?"

Max was stunned that he didn't shoot. As far as the

correctional officers were concerned, she was a cop killer. Kerns probably could have gotten away with killing her. The DA certainly wasn't going to bring him up on charges. Firing the weapon would have been ruled an *accidental discharge*, or something of that nature.

Max brought her hands into the air. She slowly turned and placed her hands against the bulkheads. The guards rushed in, wrenched her hands behind her back, and cuffed her.

One of the goons yanked her by the arm, and pulled her out of the cell. He muttered to Kerns, "You should have just killed her."

"Yeah, well, maybe next time."

Max got the impression that maybe Kerns was a decent cop. It was clear that most of the guards wouldn't think twice about killing an inmate, as long as it couldn't come back on them. But Kerns seemed to be a *by the numbers* kind of guy.

He glanced down at Junk who was writhing in agony on the deck. His body looked mangled, twisted into unnatural positions. The sergeant tapped his earbud. "I need a medical team in cellblock A-34."

The guards marched Max to an isolated unit and threw her into solitary confinement. This was where they threw the troublemakers. It was even worse than the general population. It was a small block of 16 cells, housing the worst of the worst. There was never a quiet moment in this unit. Someone was always hollering or screaming or banging their head against the bulkheads. It didn't take a person long to go stark raving mad in this place. 23 hours a day in a compartment barely large enough to stretch out in. The inmates were supposed to get an hour of recreation time in a larger solitary space, but the guards rarely afforded the prisoners that luxury. The compartments were sealed off with steel hatches. There was a slot large enough to stick a food tray through, and a small polycarbonate view port. You were lucky if you got served more than once a day.

A guard shoved Max into a cell. He followed her into the compartment and drew a stun baton from his utility belt. He was seething, and Max could see the rage behind his eyes. "You don't really think you're going to get away with killing a cop, do you?"

8

T he correctional officer was ready to give her the beating of her life. His nametape across his body armor read *B. Hoskins*. He advanced, gripping the baton tight.

Max was at a disadvantage. With her hands cuffed behind her back, she wasn't going to be able to put up much of a fight.

The other guard, Crawford, watched the show from the entry portal. This was good entertainment, and you could tell he loved watching inmates get a beat down.

Hoskins swung the baton.

Max ducked down, and the baton whooshed overhead. Max popped up and twirled a roundhouse, kicking Hoskins in the head. Her heel smacked his helmet, sending him crashing off balance into the bulkhead. Hoskins regained his composure and backhanded the baton, swinging for Max's face.

Max dodged.

The swing left Hoskins wide open, and Max planted a swift kick in his groin. Hoskins doubled over, and

Max kneed him in the face. Even through his face-mask, the blow shattered his nose. His head snapped back, and blood ran rivers from his nose, dripping down behind the mask and rolling off his chin. He fell back against the bulkhead and collapsed to the deck.

His baton was resting across his leg, teetering like a seesaw. Max stomped the end of it, launching the baton into the air, twirling like it had been thrown from a majorette in a marching band.

Max spun around and caught the baton behind her back. Everything happened in a flash. Her ruthless gaze found Crawford's terrified eyes. He hovered in the portal, frozen with fear. It had all happened so fast, he didn't have time to react. Even with her hands cuffed behind her back, Max was proving she was more than capable of inflicting damage.

Crawford mashed a button on the bulkhead and slammed the hatch shut as fast as he could. The heavy steel hatch clamored throughout the cellblock. Max heard the locking mechanism latch shut.

Crawford sprinted down the corridor and mashed the alarm button on the bulkhead. Klaxons blared throughout the prison pod. The grating sound was ear piercing. It wouldn't be long before the emergency response team flooded the cellblock.

Max dropped to the deck and searched Hoskins for keys. She found a pair and was able to release the cuffs —first from one hand, then the other. She tossed them aside and snatched Hoskins's STN-60 from its holster. She pulled the groggy guard to his feet and placed the weapon to his temple. By this time, Crawford was back at the hatch, peering wide-eyed through the viewport.

"Unlock the hatch, or I'm going to scramble his brain."

Crawford didn't know what the hell to do.

Several more guards flooded into the corridor, deactivated the blaring alarms, and surrounded the cell.

"I mean it. I've got nothing to lose," Max shouted. "Open the hatch, now! He won't be able to wipe his ass if I pull this trigger."

"Just take it easy," Sergeant Kerns yelled through the hatch.

"I'm going to count to three. One… Two…"

"Okay. Okay," Kerns said. "I'm unlocking the hatch."

Max heard the locking mechanism click. A moment later, the hatch slid open. The instant it did, one of the guards fired a disruptor pulse at Max. The shot instantly made Hoskins's body go limp and fall to the deck. Max had been using him as cover—now she was completely vulnerable.

Max stayed on her feet, albeit a little dazed from the neural disruptor.

The guard fired two more pulses, and the rest of the response team stormed the compartment.

Max was caught in a foggy brain haze. It was like having a senior moment—like walking into a room and forgetting why you came in there in the first place.

Max managed to pull herself out of it as the goons rushed toward her. She fired off several disruptor pulses, taking out the entire squad. Their bodies covered the deck.

Max stripped Hoskins of his clothing and tactical armor. She suited up, placed the helmet and face-mask on her head, and stepped over the fallen bodies in the corridor.

The uniform was too big for her. But at a quick glance, she might pass for a correctional officer. But the subterfuge wouldn't last long. The bigger problem was going to be getting out of the high security solitary confinement unit. The segregated area was secured by a biometric scanner pad. Only palm prints of correctional officers on the current schedule could open the secure hatches.

Max grabbed Sergeant Kerns's wrist and placed the palm of her hand against his. She pressed the two together for a moment, sampling his skin, then ran down the corridor to the entry hatch. Max was no ordinary human.

The raucous hoots and hollers of the prisoners spilled into the corridor. They were like caged animals in a zoo going crazy. They knew something was happening, and they were thrilled about it.

Max placed her hand on the pad—an instant later, the hatch unlocked and slid open. She ran through the hallway, back to the main pod. As she stepped into the common area, she ran into another squad of emergency response officers—four angry goons in full riot gear, looking to crack skulls. This was probably as far as Max was going to get.

9

"Hurry! Officers down!" Max yelled. "They've taken over solitary."

The emergency response team rushed down the hallway toward the solitary confinement unit without a second thought.

Max breathed a sigh of relief. Her heart was racing, and she was sweating under the thick armor. She moved briskly through the common area of the prison pod, heading for the exit. When she reached the first security checkpoint, she placed her hand on the biometric scanner. An indicator light blinked green, and the hatch slid open.

Max stepped through, and the hatch clanked shut behind her. She was more nervous now. One more security checkpoint to go through, then an easy stroll through the intake area, and she'd be free. She casually marched past correction officers in the command center as they monitored the situation. They were too distracted to pay much attention to Max.

She reached the second security checkpoint and

placed her hand on the scanner. But nothing happened. The indicator light stayed red. Either her cover was blown, she had lost the pattern of Sergeant Kerns's hand print, or the final gate was on lockdown due to the security crisis.

One of the guards in the control room glanced at her with a quizzical look on his face.

Max waved at him.

He hesitated a moment, then pressed a button on a control terminal.

The light flashed green, and the hatch to the last checkpoint slid open. Max stepped through the portal and strolled down the corridor toward the main exit. There were no more security checkpoints. She was practically home free. She made her way past the reception desk and was only a few feet from the exit hatch when her hope of freedom came crashing down.

"That's far enough," the warden said.

Max stopped in her tracks. She had the eerie feeling that a weapon was pointed at her. And her feelings were never wrong.

"Put your hands in the air and turn around slowly."

Max did as the warden commanded. She was face-to-face with the business end of a plasma pistol. She was quickly surrounded by several armed tactical officers—the barrels of angry rifles staring her in the face.

"Slowly take off your helmet," the warden said.

Max complied. She shook out her hair and took a deep breath. Her raven black hair glistened like a shampoo commercial. The air inside the helmet was stuffy, and her cheeks were slick with a thin mist of sweat.

"I've got to hand it to you, that was some impressive

work. No one has ever escaped from this prison facility. And no one ever will. At least, not on my watch."

"Go ahead and shoot me. Because I'm not going back in there."

"I find myself in a bit of a predicament. Part of me wants to kill you. Chace Carter was a good friend. And I would like nothing more than to squeeze this trigger and watch you fry. But then the other part of me thinks that would be too easy. A lifetime of misery in a maximum-security slam seems more fitting. For that reason, I'm going to keep you alive. Besides, you haven't been convicted yet, and I'm going to give you the benefit of the doubt."

"I don't think the rest of your staff got the memo."

"You'll be moved to a special protective custody unit."

Max scoffed. "I've seen your idea of protective custody."

"I'll assign guards to you that I know to be of high moral caliber."

Max chuckled. "High moral caliber? In a place like this."

"Some of us are here because we believe in the law. Besides, it seems the FCIS has taken an interest in you. An agent is on his way to personally interrogate you. I've been instructed to make sure you are fully capable of attending that interview."

Max had a puzzled look on her face. "What interest does the Federation have in a local matter?"

The warden shrugged. "Orion Station is in Federation space. We fall under the purview of multiple Federation agencies, including the Criminal Investigative Service. Believe me, the OPD will squabble over jurisdictional issues. But they can't keep the Feds from talking to you."

Max was of two minds on the subject. Perhaps an impartial Federation agent might be more willing to listen to her story than a local cop with a knee-jerk response. But, given her background, an incident like this could stir up a knee-jerk reaction from the Federation as well. And she was on shaky ground with the Federation as it was.

"I don't suppose you'd be interested in telling me how you made it past our security checkpoints?" the warden asked.

Max gave him a sly smirk.

10

The warden wasn't taking any chances. Max was in handcuffs and leg irons. A neural ring was affixed around her head. It was a narrow band that she wore like a halo. The contact pads pressed against her temples. In theory, the neural ring could create cognitive disruption at the press of a remote. The frequency and intensity was fully adjustable. But since Max had failed to respond to the STN-60s, the warden wasn't putting much stock into the neural ring. He also heavily sedated her in an attempt to make her more docile.

She sat in an interrogation room across from the FCIS agent. He was anything but impartial. Rage boiled under his skin. His steely eyes pierced into her like lasers. It looked like he was doing everything he could to hold himself back. His hands were trembling, he was so angry.

"I'm going to ask you one more time—"

"I'm telling you, you've got the wrong girl," Max said casually.

The agent took a deep breath and held it, trying to calm himself down. He had a square jaw, dark hair, and looked like he kept himself fit.

"You're kinda cute when you're angry," Max said, messing with him.

It sent him through the roof. He scowled at her. "You know, before I joined the agency, I was in the Navy. Special Warfare."

"Good for you," Max said.

"Strategic Intelligence Command. One of my jobs was to procure intelligence from live assets."

"Is that supposed to intimidate me?"

"It should. I am very skilled at extracting information from people."

"Give it your best shot. I've already told you everything you need to know. I didn't kill Chace Carter. And every minute you spend dicking around in here with me is time wasted. I'm sure you're aware of the statistics. If a crime isn't solved in the first 48, it's probably not going to be. And, by my count, you're running out of time."

The agent's face tensed. He didn't want to hear it. "Don't say I didn't warn you. We could have done this the easy way." He started to reach for his briefcase resting on the deck, but was interrupted.

"Have you even taken a look at the evidence? Eyewitness testimony from a cop Carter was probably banging? No other physical evidence? Conveniently missing surveillance footage that could prove my innocence? If you don't smell something funny, then you're not very good at your job, Agent... I'm sorry, you never mentioned your name?"

"Carter. Dylan Carter."

Max put it all together. "Chace was your brother."

"You catch on quick. Now you know this is personal for me."

"Well, if you want to find your brother's killer, you're going to need to pull your head out of your ass and start looking in the right place."

Dylan clenched his jaw.

"Look, do you just want to lock someone up to make you feel better, or do you want real justice?"

"Okay. Why don' t you start by telling me who you are? I mean, that's a pretty handy trick not to show up in the Federation database. I don' t know anybody who can do that except..." Dylan suddenly had a realization. His eyes narrowed at her, studying her features intensely. "Tell me about your military background."

"I never said I was in the military."

"You didn't have to. I saw the footage of your attempted escape. The way you handled yourself... My first thought was special operator. Navy Reaper. Maybe Space Corps Recon. "

Max said nothing.

"I watched how you bypassed the security checkpoints. What did you use? A simple bio-film on your hand to sample the guard's palm print? A pretty common tool among intel agents and special operators."

Max said nothing.

Dylan reached into his pocket and placed a small device on the table. It was no more than an inch or two in diameter. Dylan pressed a button and activated the device. "I'm sure you know what this is?"

Max nodded.

The audio and video recording of the interrogation room was instantly scrambled.

Detective Reese was in the viewing room watching through the two-way mirror. He grumbled to himself. "Goddamn Feds." He knew damn good and well what Dylan had done. He marched out of the compartment and opened the hatch to the interrogation room. He flashed an insincere smile and spoke in a congenial tone. "We lost audio feed," he said, playing ignorant. "I've got my tech people working to solve the issue. Maybe you could pause interrogation for a few moments. If we can't resolve the problem, perhaps we can move you to Interrogation 3?"

"No need. My line of questioning is going to veer into classified territory. You understand. I'll restore audio and video shortly."

Reese forced another smile. "Excellent. Glad to know our equipment isn't faulty." He lingered in the portal for moment.

"Thank you, Detective Reese. That'll be all."

Reese shut the hatch, and his smile instantly faded. He marched back to the observation room. He might not have been able to hear what they were saying, but he was going to watch anyway.

Dylan grabbed his briefcase from the deck and set it on the table. He unlatched it and lifted the lid. Inside were instruments to aid with enhanced interrogation techniques. He pulled out a device and set it on the table. It resembled a small remote control. It had a few buttons and a dial. "This is one of my favorite toys," he said with a devious grin.

He didn't have to explain to Max what it was. She already knew.

"I can send simulated pain impulses straight to your brain through that ring on your head. I find it particularly effective. And the beauty is, it doesn't leave any marks or permanent damage. Oh, sure, its use has been banned by the *Galactic Convention*, but it's going to be your word against mine."

Max didn't show a hint of concern on her face.

"I can dial this thing up to 10, but I usually start with less than 1. Most people don't make it past 2. Occasionally, someone will make it to 3—usually a woman. They seem to be tougher than men. It's funny, some of the biggest guys crack before I even get to level 1."

Max grinned. "Want to place a bet on how much I can take? Why don't we make this interesting?"

"What do you have in mind?"

11

Max grimaced with pain. Every nerve in her body was on fire. It felt like her skin was being branded with a hot iron. She felt jolts of pain emanating from deep within her bones and joints. Dylan had ratcheted the device up to level 4 already. His eyes were wide with disbelief.

Max was able to attenuate the nerve impulses. She was well aware of the discomfort, but with a little concentration, she was able to reduce the sensation to little more than a minor irritation.

Dylan turned the dial to 5.

The spike of pain hurt for a moment. A thin mist of sweat formed on her cheeks, and her heartbeat elevated. Then Max was able to dial it down in her mind.

Dylan let the device run for a few moments. He was stunned.

"Is that all you got?"

Dylan grimaced and finally shut the device off. "I've never seen anybody take that much pain."

"Mind over matter."

"I think it's more than that."

"Are you going to hold to our deal, or not?"

Dylan didn't look pleased that he had lost the bet. He had figured it was a sure thing. "You have no record. You're highly trained. You exhibit an extreme resistance to pain. I know what you are."

"What am I?" Max said with a smug grin.

"The result of a collaboration between the United Intelligence Agency and Naval Special Warfare. Project SW Ultra. A genetically engineered unit of elite special warfare operators. As I recall, the project was scrapped after some rather unfortunate incidents. But I thought all of the operators were dead?"

"Not all. There are a few of us still out there. But if I have any say in the matter, there's going to be one less."

Dylan's eyes narrowed at her, confused. "So you admitting your intention to murder an SW Ultra operator? That doesn't do much to bolster your assertion that you're an upstanding member of the community."

"Call it galactic justice. Somebody needs to pay for what happened to Doctor Tor." Max was visibly upset at the memory. Her eyes brimmed slightly.

"SW Ultra was a project that never should have been started."

Max's eyes blazed into him. "Doctor Tor was like a father to me."

"Don't expect me to have much sympathy for a trained killer that was grown in a lab. You're a genetic abomination."

Max's eyes narrowed, and the scowl on her face became more pronounced.

"I bet the UIA would love to know your whereabouts. Your suspected involvement in the death of a law enforcement officer would be quite embarrassing for them. I'm sure they'd want you terminated. I can see the headlines now. *Former covert experiment gone wrong! UIA assassin goes on civilian killing spree!*"

"Technically, not a spree killing. And I haven't killed anyone aboard the station. Yet." Max arched an eyebrow at him. "You seem like a smart guy, why don't you use that brain of yours to do some critical thinking. I don't want you to hurt yourself or anything, but just think about this for a moment. Now that you know my background, do you really think I would have been so sloppy about the way the crime scene was handled. Chace was killed in a public restroom. Not a location I would have picked. And you think I'd linger around in a terminal bar waiting to get picked up by local PD? I would have been in and out before the body hit the ground."

Dylan pondered this.

"Maybe that's your alibi. Commit the crime in such a sloppy fashion that no one in their right mind would think it was committed by an elite special warfare operator."

Max rolled her eyes. "Okay, maybe I gave you too much credit when I called you *smart*."

Dylan frowned.

"There was a guy that hit on me at the bar." Max searched for his name. "Tim. Grab the passenger manifests. He shouldn't be too hard to find." Max pondered this for a moment. "On second thought, he's married. He's probably going to deny everything. But go to *Plasmatronics*. Start investigating."

"Any witnesses who were there are going to be halfway across the galaxy by now."

"Start with the bartender," Max said, dryly. "This is *Investigations 101.*"

Dylan glared at her.

"We had a deal. I survived your little torture device. Now you have to start looking at this case objectively."

Dylan was silent a moment. He pushed away from the table and stood up. He grabbed the jamming device from the table and deactivated it. Then closed his briefcase containing the torture implements. "I'll look into it. Don't go anywhere," he said with a sardonic tone.

"LEARN ANYTHING USEFUL?" Detective Reese asked as Dylan stepped out of the interrogation room.

Dylan shrugged. "We'll see."

Reese stopped him as he started to walk away. "Did she say anything about the robot?"

"What robot?"

"Your brother's personal service bot. Winston. He's been missing. We believe he may have more evidence and might be able to shed some light on motive."

"She didn't say anything about a robot. But the suspect did bring up some interesting questions... What motive would she have for killing my brother?"

Reese shrugged. "That's why we're hoping to find the robot. Perhaps the suspect was having an affair with Chace. Who knows? Crime of passion?"

Dylan politely nodded and turned away.

Reese called after him, "You know, in my detective

work, I find it's always best to separate the *why* from the *how*."

Dylan glanced back at him, a little perplexed. "I've always found if you understand the *why*, you can figure out the *how*."

Dylan made his way out of the station and navigated the maze of corridors to Chace's apartment. The size of the station was overwhelming, and was easy to get lost in. Dylan slid the key card into the lock, and the access light flashed green. The hatch slid open, and a gust of air flowed into the corridor. It smelled like Chace. A faint trace of his cologne still lingered in the air. Dylan felt his knees wobble. His heart sank into his stomach, heavy with loss. It was hard to believe Chace was gone. Dylan tried to stand tall and took a deep breath before he stepped into his brother's apartment.

The lighting flickered on automatically. The apartment had been ransacked. Drawers rummaged through, clothing scattered on the deck, shelves demolished. Someone had been looking for something. It became clear that Chace's death wasn't just a random act of violence.

12

"It's a good thing you like music," Dylan said through the hatch.

Max was lying on a bunk in a protective custody cell. She sat up at the sound of Dylan's voice. She heard the locking mechanism unlatch, and the hatch slid open.

Dylan stood in the portal. "Well, are you going to stay in there? I'm sure that can be arranged, but you might have to start paying rent."

Max's eyes widened.

"You're free to go." Dylan said slowly, as if speaking to someone who didn't understand the language.

Max hopped off the bunk and stepped into the corridor. "You don't have to tell me twice."

"Apparently, I did."

She arched an eyebrow at him.

"The entertainment bot at *Plasmatronics* has time-stamped video footage of you purchasing a song around the time of the murder. Unless you can be at two places at the same time, I think that pretty much proves your innocence." Dylan escorted her out of the protective custody wing, down a corridor, and across the general population pod. "It would seem I owe you an apology."

"Apology accepted. I guess I should say thank you."

"No need to thank me. I need to be thanking you. Convicting the wrong person wouldn't have done justice for my brother. And I said some pretty harsh things to you in the interrogation room."

"Oh, you mean like calling me a genetic abomination? Pfft. Flattery will get you nowhere. Insults are the way to a girl's heart." Her voice was dripping with sarcasm.

Dylan cringed. "Probably not my finest moment."

The other prisoners hooted and hollered as Max marched toward the exit. Every time an inmate got released, it was like a triumph for everyone. Despite their differences, they liked to see each other beat the system.

But the correctional officers didn't share the same enthusiasm. Max was met with the unforgiving glares of guards as she passed. There may have been evidence to exonerate her, but the OPD wasn't happy about it. They were back to square one with no suspects.

"What are you going to do now?" Dylan asked.

"I'm going to get as far away from Orion Station as possible. Then I'm going to keep looking for that son-of-a-bitch that killed Doctor Tor."

Dylan paused for a moment, trying to figure out the best way to make his pitch. Then he just blurted it out. "I was thinking that perhaps you might stay for a few days."

Max didn't like the idea one iota, and the look she

gave him made it painfully obvious. "Why the hell would I do something like that?"

"My brother's apartment was ransacked. He contacted me a few days before his death. Said he needed to share information with me, but didn't feel safe sending it over the network. Said I needed to come here and meet him in person. Now he's dead. Someone was looking for something in his apartment."

"What does this have to do with me?"

"You have a certain skill set. And I could use some assistance."

"That's what the OPD is for."

"I find that I'm getting a little resistance," Dylan said. "I get the impression that they don't particularly like a Fed sticking his nose in their business."

"Not surprising."

"I would pay you, of course, for your time."

"You want to hire me as a private investigator?"

"Something like that."

Max looked at him like he was crazy. "That's not exactly in my line of work."

"Don't sell yourself short. I did some digging. It took some work, but I was able to pull the files of every project SW Ultra member. You're highly skilled at gathering and analyzing intelligence. Identifying and neutralizing threats. I feel confident that you would make a valuable asset."

"The UIA might argue otherwise."

"Take a day. Think about it. I'll set you up at the finest hotel on Orion Station—if you choose to stay."

Max looked into his eyes and tried to size him up. It was an odd request. Yesterday he wanted to see her hang, today he was begging her to be a partner.

"Listen, I'm really sorry about your brother. I appreciate you digging up the footage from that entertainment bot. But I'm not sticking around this place any longer than I have to."

Dylan frowned. "I understand."

The warden greeted them at the last security checkpoint. He flashed a smile. "Well, it seems that I have misjudged you."

"I want my pistol returned. You don't expect a girl to travel across the galaxy without one, now do you? Especially not with a murderer on the loose."

"Of course." He handed her a bag of her personal effects that had been confiscated upon her arrest.

Max looked in the bag and saw her pistol, ammunition, and a few jewelry items.

"You'll need to keep that in the bag until you are out of the facility. Sorry. Prison policy."

Max gave a slight nod of agreement.

"I hope you will accept our most sincere apology for the inconvenience. Here's a transport voucher to anywhere in the galaxy, courtesy of the OPD. No hard feelings."

Max took the voucher. The warden waited for a *thank you*, but he never got one. He finally forced a smile again and said, "Safe journey."

The warden opened the hatch to the last security checkpoint. Max and Dylan stepped through, and the hatch slid shut behind them. All Max had to do was walk 15 feet to the main exit, and the prison pod on Orion Station was going to be a memory. She was going to make a beeline for the terminal and take the first transport out. She didn't care where it was going. Anyplace was better than this place.

Max held her hand out to Dylan. "Best of luck."

Dylan shook her hand, then dug out a business card. He handed her the thin piece of smart glass. "Take this. Call me if you change your mind."

"Don't get your hopes up."

Max spun around and Dylan watched her strut toward the main exit. "By the way. I may be able to help you find Silas Rage."

Max stopped in her tracks. Now he definitely had her attention.

13

S omeone was following Max. She knew how to spot a tail. She kept thinking about Dylan's offer as she strolled down the hallway, heading for the transport terminal. Help him solve his brother's murder in exchange for access to the UIA database and any known whereabouts of Silas Rage. It was an enticing offer. Rage had been responsible for the death of Doctor Tor, and the downfall of the SW Ultra program. He was on the most wanted list, but he had proven to be quite elusive. After all, the Ultras had been trained to hide in plain sight. They were phantoms.

A bald man in civilian clothing trailed behind Max by 30 yards. She noticed him shortly after she left the prison pod. He was a cop. No doubt about it. As she crossed the next junction, she picked up another tail. He fell in line behind her, pretending to read from a tablet. The bald man turned off on another junction, while the reader drifted along. The new follower wore dark sunglasses and a backwards ball-cap. Wearing sunglasses on Orion Station was like wearing snow-shoes at the beach.

Max kept weaving through the maze of passage-ways until she reached the departure terminal. There were crowds of people coming and going. Travelers in all shapes and sizes from all over the galaxy. There were overstuffed bags and frantic passengers rushing to make connections.

The man following her loitered around a coffee kiosk, keeping an eye on her.

Max scanned the area. Her eyes fixed on a young woman about the same age and build. She had blonde hair, and her head was down, glued to her mobile device. She was texting away a storm.

Max made a beeline for her and introduced herself. "Hi, I'm Max," she said, offering a hand.

The blonde woman looked up from her mobile with a quizzical look on her face. "Uh, hi," she stammered. "I'm Abigail." She had no idea why Max was intro-ducing herself. It all seemed a bit odd.

Max shook the woman's hand and smiled. "Well, it was nice to meet you. I've got to run."

"Um, okay."

Max walked away, and the woman went back to her phone and made a face. "Weirdness," she muttered to herself.

Max strolled to the ticketing counter. She glanced around to see if anyone was watching her. The man that had been following her was sipping a cup of coffee. A redhead in a tight black dress had gotten his attention. He lowered his sunglasses and his eyes followed the woman's assets as she sauntered up to the barista.

Max shook her hair out. It flowed like a shampoo

commercial and transformed color from raven black to blonde. The same color as Abigail's hair.

Max continued to the ticketing counter. "What's the first transport out of here?" Max asked the agent.

"I've got a flight to Bellatrix 6 that you might be able to catch, if you hurry."

"I'll take it." Max handed her the ticket voucher.

"Is that round-trip? Or one-way?"

"One way. I'm never coming back here again."

"I'm sorry you didn't have a pleasant stay." The agent leaned in and whispered. "I'll see if I can bump you up to first class." The ticketing agent smiled and winked.

"Thank you. That would be nice."

"I'll just need to verify your ID."

Max placed her hand on the bio scanner. An instant later, Abigail Matheson's picture and information appeared on the agent's screen. With a handshake, Max had sampled a woman's palm print.

"Alright, Abigail," the agent said. "You are all set. The flight departs in 15 minutes from gate C-23. Better hurry."

"Thank you!" Max turned around to head for the gate, but she almost ran into Mr. Sunglasses.

His face twisted up, confused. Something was different about Max, but he couldn't quite place it. He could've sworn she was a brunette.

"Is there a reason you're following me?" Max asked.

"Just making sure you get on that transport safely. We wouldn't want anything to happen to you."

It was a veiled threat. It seemed there were some in the OPD that wanted her off the station. That was fine by Max. But there was also a part of her that didn't like to be told what to do. "You know, I really didn't get to see much of Orion Station. What if I decide to stay for a few days?"

"It's a free galaxy. But I don't think that would be in your best interest."

Max liked being threatened even less than she liked being told what to do. She flashed a fake smile. "I guess it's a good thing I've got my ticket then. This place sucks anyway." She brushed past him and marched toward the gate.

She fell in line with the other passengers and hurried way down the spaceway. She settled into her cushy first-class seat, then prepared for the nine-hour quantum jump to Bellatrix 6. After a few days on a rock hard lumpy mattress, the seat felt like heaven. She reclined, almost horizontal, and Max figured she might actually get some decent sleep on this trip.

As soon as she was settled, the attendant stopped by her seat. "Can I get you a snack? Soda? Cocktail? I have beer, wine, and mixed drinks."

"Do you have Bulvacci Special Reserve?"

The attendant smiled. "Excellent choice. I'll be back with that shortly." The attendant twirled around and headed to the galley.

Max looked out the window at the cosmos. A billion glimmering stars filled the void. Max shook her hair again, and it turned back to her natural raven black. Then she lowered the tray on the seat-back in front of her. A moment later, the attendant set down a glass of smooth amber whiskey. "Enjoy!"

"I most certainly will," Max said. The attendant tilted her head and looked at Max with confusion. Not able to place what was different about her. She shrugged it off and moved onto the next row.

Max sipped the liquor, and the smooth fluid warmed her throat and heated her belly. It was the best tasting shot of whiskey she had in recent memory. Against the stark contrast of the all-purpose nutrition of the prison pod, sipping fine Antarian whiskey seemed like a dream. But something kept nagging at her. Maybe it was the cops following her to the gate, making sure she left the station. Maybe it was the opportunity to get more information about Silas Rage. Maybe it was the fact that someone had been killed, and Max couldn't quite put her finger on why.

It was none of her business, she told herself. People get killed every day all across the galaxy. Forget about it and move on. Don't get involved. That was the smart thing to do.

14

"I'm sorry ma'am, you'll need to take a seat. We're about to close the hatch and prepare for departure," the attendant said.

"Change of plans," Max said. "You can give my seat to someone else."

Max rushed through the main hatch, and down the spaceway to the terminal.

She pulled out Dylan's card and swiped the smart glass to dial his number. The call connected, and Dylan's face appeared on the small screen. He looked surprised to see Max. "Don't tell me you've changed your mind?"

"I'm not sure. But I just gave up a first-class seat, so let's talk."

"How about I meet you at *Plasmatronics*?"

"At least I know I can get a good drink there."

"See you in 15."

Max hung up, pocketed the card, and weaved her way back through the terminal. She saw the man in sunglasses that had followed her to the terminal, along with the bald guy who had initially been following her. Sunglasses shook his head and fell in alongside her. He walked with her for a few steps. "I thought you had decided to leave?"

"Flight's been delayed."

"Really? For how long?" he said with a healthy dose of skepticism.

"I haven't decided yet."

"Don't say I didn't warn you." He fell away and ambled back to the bald man. They disappeared into the crowd, but Max was sure she hadn't seen the last of them.

Plasmatronics was the same as it had been a few days earlier, only the faces had changed. A different set of weary travelers. Same hot bartender. She looked a little surprised as Max sauntered up. "Didn't expect to be seeing you again?"

"Life's full of surprises, isn't it?"

"That it is. What'll it be?"

"The usual."

The bartender chuckled. "I guess two visits makes you a regular."

Max cringed. "I never wanted to be considered a regular. Not in this crap-tastic place. No offense."

"None taken. As soon as I save up enough credits, I'm getting out of here. I've got my eye on a nice resort colony in the Alaki Nebula. Better tips, cleaner air, and closer to recreational activities."

"Sounds nice."

"I'm Skye. Nice to meet you."

"Max. Likewise." The two shook hands.

Skye returned a few moments later and slid a glass of whiskey across the bar. "This one's on the house. Try not to get arrested today," she said with a friendly wink.

"I'll do my best. No promises, though."

It didn't take long for a guy to step up to the plate and take a swing. "Is this seat taken?"

"Yes, it is," Max replied.

The guy stared at the bar stool. "I don't see anybody."

Max pointed to Dylan as he stepped into the bar.

"Lucky guy." The man flashed a courteous smile, then strolled away, dejected.

Dylan's eyes made contact with Max. He marched across the bar, taking the empty seat next to her.

"Can I get you anything?" Skye asked.

"Bottle of water," Dylan said.

Maxed arched a curious eyebrow at him.

"I'm on the job. Federal agents can't just have cocktails while investigating."

"Sucks to be you." Max took a sip of her whiskey.

"Listen, thank you for staying."

"Don't thank me yet. Right now, I'm just delaying my departure. But one thing is for sure, there are some members of the OPD that don't want me around." Max paused for a moment. "Do you have any idea what your brother was working on? Anybody who might want him dead?"

"He wouldn't talk about specifics, even on an encrypted channel. And I'm getting massive pushback from the OPD. They're not letting me anywhere near the case."

"Can't you pull some strings? You're pretty high up in *the company*."

Dylan hesitated a moment. "It's a delicate situation.

Technically homicide of a local police officer on Orion Station is not a Federation matter. The local authorities have jurisdiction. But Chace wasn't just an OPD officer."

Max had a quizzical look on her face. "Explain."

Dylan glanced around the bar to make sure no one was paying any attention to them. Then he leaned in and whispered, "My brother was an FCIS agent."

"So he was working undercover?"

Dylan nodded.

"The murder of a Federation agent gives you jurisdiction."

"Yes, it also blows his cover and let's everyone know the FCIS is snooping around."

"What was he looking for? Corruption within the OPD? That doesn't seem like a Federation concern."

"That's classified."

Max rolled her eyes. "How do you expect me to help you if you're not going to tell me everything?"

Dylan said nothing.

Max gulped her drink down and pushed away from the bar. "Good luck. I'm outta here."

Max strutted away. Dylan grimaced, then called after her. "Wait!"

Max craned her neck back and arched an eyebrow at him.

"Have a seat."

Max slid her perfect ass back on the barstool. "Skye, can we get another round. This one's on my friend here."

"Sure thing."

Max's crystal eyes found Dylan. "You were saying?"

15

"I think, perhaps, we should take this conversation somewhere else," Max said, eyeing the two OPD officers that entered the bar. They were in full tactical gear carrying plasma rifles. But they weren't moving with urgency. Max watched as they made note of her, but that was it. They didn't seem to be here to arrest her. Nonetheless, Max didn't want to hang around for them to change their minds.

"We can go back to my hotel," Dylan said. "I'm staying at the Plaza."

"Don't get any funny ideas. We're just going to discuss the case."

"Of course. I wasn't implying anything else."

Max arched an eyebrow at him.

"Don't flatter yourself. You are *so* not my type."

Max was everyone's type.

Dylan's suite at the Plaza was luxurious. Panoramic windows offered a stunning view of the surrounding cosmos. The Lotar nebula wasn't far away, and made for a nice view.

The living area was impeccably decorated. There was a couch, coffee table, entertainment center, minibar, and a kitchenette. Max figured Dylan was getting the company to spring for it.

I see the FCIS is treating you well," Max said. She strolled to the minibar and perused the selection of liquor, then poured herself another drink.

"They're pretty generous with my expense account."

"You want one?" She said, offering to fix him a drink. Dylan shook his head.

"Oh, that's right. On-the-job."

"Do you ever slow down?"

"I metabolize this stuff really fast. The downside of being a *genetic freak*, as you would say." She couldn't help but throw his previous comment back in his face. "I have to drink a whole lot to feel anything, and the effects don't last that long."

"So, you're not a cheap date?"

"Not at all." Max moved to the window and took in the view.

Dylan couldn't help but check her out. She was definitely a sight to behold. "Tell me more."

"More about what?"

"You. How are you able to sample fingerprints? Morph your hair color?"

"You need to ask Doctor Tor those questions. I don't know how I can do what I do, it just comes natural. I can change my hair color, my eye color, replicate biometric attributes. Comes in handy for passing retinal scans, and fingerprint IDs...even voice analysis. You have to remember, one of my main functions was to infiltrate and eliminate high-value targets."

"Impressive."

"I can't shape-shift or anything like that. I think that was something Doctor Tor was working on for the next generation."

"Doctor Tor designed your genetic code from scratch, am I right?"

Max nodded.

"It seems he was beginning to blur the lines."

Max shot him a look.

"I mean, one could argue that you're a biosynthetic humanoid."

"I'm flesh and blood, just like you."

"Not exactly like me. Your tissue regenerates faster. According to the files, you don't age."

Max shrugged. "I haven't noticed any signs of aging myself, but I have a termination date."

Dylan lifted a curious eyebrow.

"It's programmed into the genetic code of all the Ultras. One day, our DNA will just start to unravel."

"Do you know how long?"

Max shook her head. "Maybe a year. Maybe 5. Maybe 50. Who knows?" Isn't it in the files?"

"No," Dylan said.

Max shrugged. "I'll probably die from a bullet long before then."

"So, you're an optimist?" Dylan said with more than a trace of sarcasm.

Max paused for a moment, reflecting on her past. "I've been technically dead before. It's taught me to cherish every moment."

"What was that like?"

Her eyes flared and she spoke in a dramatic tone. "There was a big bright light, and a calm soothing voice called out to me. You want to know what the voice said?"

Dylan nodded.

"It said stay away from Orion Station."

Dylan sneered at her for pulling his leg.

"So what was your brother doing here?"

Dylan paused a moment. "We believe weapons are being moved through this facility, supplying insurgent terrorists. We placed Chace undercover to investigate. The idea being that a local detective sniffing around wouldn't draw much attention as a Federation Security Agent. If we put too much pressure on them, the whole operation might just disappear and start up somewhere else."

"Do you think OPD officers are involved?"

Dylan shrugged. "It's hard to say. Could be somebody within the department. Could be somebody within the customs enforcement agency. Or it could be any number of organized crime elements that are operating on the station."

"Or it could be that his girlfriend caught him cheating and she decided to teach him a lesson."

Dylan shook his head. "Chace was a decent guy. Loyal."

"Have you talked to the girlfriend?"

"She won't talk to me. Like I said, the OPD isn't too keen on a Fed poking his nose around their business. They want to handle it internally." Dylan paused. "I don't blame them, really. If a cop gets killed, the rest of the department is out for blood."

"Tell me about it."

"We need to find his service bot, Winston. He may have some information."

"Good luck. Your brother was getting too close to something," Max said. "If Winston has any damning information, I can guarantee you he's in a million pieces right now and probably got hauled off the station in the last trash dump."

"I hope you're wrong."

"I'm almost never wrong."

Dylan gave her a look.

"We need to get a list of his open cases. Find out who he was digging into."

"Our best shot is the girlfriend." Dylan looked at Max, expectantly. But Max didn't have any answers.

"She's not going to talk to me."

16

"**M**ind if I have a seat?" Max asked.

Officer Calhoun's eyes burned into her. "You've got a lot of nerve coming around here."

Lockup was a cop bar not far from the OPD head-quarters. Max had been met with unfriendly stares from the moment she stepped inside. Officer Calhoun was sitting at the bar with red puffy eyes and a solemn face. The half-empty glass of beer in front of her wasn't her first one.

Max took a seat next to her. She motioned to the bartender, "Bring her another round, on me."

Mayor Thornton was on TV boasting about the low crime rates on Orion Station, and the high job opportunities. How Orion was poised to be the next great mega-lopolis, now that the economy was expanding with unprecedented year-over-year growth. He was trying to counter the bad press that had come with the recent murder.

The bartender slid a fresh beer in front of Officer

Calhoun. She slugged her old one down, then grabbed the new one and marched away. She took a seat at a nearby table.

Max paid the tab and followed after her.

"What do you want?"

"I want the same thing you want. To find out who killed Chace."

"You've already been cleared, why do you care?"

Max sat down next to her. "Exactly. I've been cleared. That means whoever killed Chace is still out there. And if you don't care about seeing them brought to justice, by all means, don't talk to me." Max stood up and walked away.

"Wait."

Max stopped and looked back at Officer Calhoun. The officer motioned for her to have a seat. Max returned to the table and sat down. There was a long silence between them.

"Why did you lie?"

"I didn't lie." Calhoun paused a long moment. Her eyes brimmed, still emotional. She took a deep breath and decided to come clean. "We were in the shopping district, not far from the terminal. I ducked into a boutique to look at some cute tops and Chace went down the hall to use a public restroom. When he didn't come back, I went looking for him. I bumped into a woman in the hallway, scurrying away from the restrooms. I didn't think much of it at first. In my recollection, she looked a lot like you." She hung her head, shameful. "Reese assured me that you were the perpetrator. He said he had seen the surveillance video before it was corrupted. I wasn't about to let a conviction slide away."

"Can you think of anybody who wanted Chace dead?"

"Every cop makes enemies."

"Was he investigating anything in particular?"

"Don't you think the OPD's already been through this? Why don't you just let local law enforcement do their job?"

"Because it doesn't seem like they are very good at it. No offense."

"What's your interest in this anyway?"

"Somebody tried to set me up to take the fall. I'd kind of like to find out who that is, and why."

There was a moment of silence between them. Calhoun looked over Max, trying to size her up.

"It's clear that someone wanted this case wrapped up quickly. Someone doesn't want this case investigated. You find out who that is, you'll find the killer."

"How dare you come in here and accuse the OPD of corruption?"

Max shrugged. "If the shoe fits..." She stood up. "I'll be at the Plaza if you can think of anything useful."

Max ambled out of the bar and made her way through the maze of passageways, heading back toward the Plaza.

Two men were following her. There wasn't much traffic in this section of the station and they stuck out like sore thumbs.

Max turned a corner at the next junction and was met with a pipe to the belly. Two thugs had been waiting for her. The hard steel mashed her abdomen, doubling her over with pain. She gasped for breath as the thugs hovered over her. The pipe crashed down again, slamming against her back, cracking ribs. The impact flattened her against the deck and sent a jolt through her spine.

A hard boot slammed into her jaw as another thug kicked her. Her lips split, and the metallic tinny taste of blood filled her mouth. The force of the impact wrenched her neck to the side, splattering the bulkhead with crimson blood.

The two goons that had been following her caught up. She was now surrounded by four thugs taking turns planting boots into her rib cage. Each kick mangled her internal organs, and the contents of her stomach crept up into the back of her throat. Deep pain filled every fiber of her being. Max tried to dial it down in her mind, but it still was unpleasant.

"You should have left when you had the chance," one of them muttered.

The hard pipe crashed down again with brutal force. Max reached her hand up to block it. Her metacarpals fractured as she wrapped her palm around the pipe, deflecting the blow.

She lunged the pipe forward, plowing it into the thug's belly. He hunched over, the contents of his stomach begging to get out.

Max yanked back, stripping the pipe from his grasp. She sprang to her feet, swinging the pipe around. The heavy steel cracked one of the goons in the head, shattering his orbital bone. He fell to the deck, unconscious. The foothills of a small mountain grew on his face, swollen and bruised from the impact. Dark purple circles formed under his eyes, and his scleras filled with blood. The laceration on his cheek was a chasm that oozed blood onto the deck. He wasn't getting up anytime soon.

17

One of the other thugs lunged for Max. But it didn't work out too well for him. He got an up close and personal introduction to Max's boot as it cracked him in the face from a roundhouse kick. The blow knocked him into the bulkhead. He staggered on his feet a moment before collapsing.

The last thug took off running. He didn't want any part of this.

Max wiped the blood from her chin on her sleeve. Then she pulled out her mobile device and took pictures of the goons lying on the ground for reference. She wanted to know who they were.

She threw the pipe on the deck and headed back to the Plaza.

Dylan's wide eyes gazed at her in shock as he pulled the door open to his suite. "What the hell happened to you?"

"Just making new friends." Max hobbled into the room, making a beeline for the minibar. But instead of making a drink, she scooped ice into a glass and pressed it against her face. Her once smooth skin was now scuffed and raw, colored multiple shades of purple, green, yellow, and blue.

"We need to get you to the med center."

Max ambled to the couch and sat down. She winced with every step. "Not necessary. I'm fine."

"You don't look fine."

"You should see the other guys."

"I can imagine," Dylan said. "Do you have any idea who it was?"

"I've got pictures. You can run them through the database. I'll transfer them to your mobile." She pulled out her phone and sent the images to Dylan.

Max's hand was swollen like a softball. She could barely wiggle her fingers, and the throbbing pain shot up her arm to meet her aching jaw and neck. Each breath was like a knife stabbing through her thoracic cavity. Cracked ribs were no fun.

"I really think you need to get looked at."

"Give it time. I will regenerate. I heal faster, remember."

"If you say so."

Max laid back on the couch rotating the glass of ice between her various points of injury. "You don't happen to have any cryo-gel, do you?"

"I bet they have some in the med center."

Max sneered at him.

"Okay, fine. Suit yourself. You want to sit around here and be uncomfortable, be my guest." Dylan left her on the couch to wallow in her own misery.

He ran the images of Max's attackers' through the FCIS database. It didn't take long to come up with a hit. The attackers' images, along with their full background record and criminal history, appeared on Dylan's screen. "Those weren't cops."

Max's brow crinkled with surprise.

"We're not talking about pristine angels here. Looks like they've all got rap sheets as long as the Otari Nebula. I'm having the system cross-reference now."

A holographic image of the concierge appeared. "Mr. Carter. An officer Calhoun is here to see you. Should I send her up to your suite?"

Dylan exchanged a surprised glance with Max. What the hell was she doing here? Surely she hadn't changed her mind?

"Uh, sure," Dylan stammered. "Send her up."

"Very well."

"Thank you."

The concierge bowed and the hologram vanished.

Dylan waited for the results of the cross-reference on his mobile. The system displayed a list of interconnected associates among the assailants. They were listed in descending order based on relevance. "Joe Duke."

"Who's that?"

"According to this, he's one of the biggest crime bosses in the Zeta Epsilon sector. He's been brought up on charges of narcotics trafficking, racketeering, extortion, murder—but none of it has been able to stick. All of those goons that attacked you have ties to him."

Max perked up, and a slight grin crawled on her lips. "Sounds like he warrants further investigation."

There was a knock at the door. Calhoun's image appeared on the view screen attached to the door. It was a nice security touch that allowed the occupant to see visitors, along with a wide section of the hallway.

Dylan strode to the door and pulled it open.

Calhoun looked uncomfortable. She glanced down the hallway in all directions, making sure she wasn't followed. "Mind if I come in?"

Dylan swung the door wide and stepped aside. He gestured for her to enter with his hand. "By all means."

Calhoun stepped into the suite, taking in the luxurious appointments. Her eyes found Max, and a wave of concern washed over her face. "What happened?"

"It seems somebody doesn't much care for me asking questions," Max said.

"Did this happen after you left the bar?"

Max nodded.

"Does the name Joe Duke mean anything to you?" Dylan asked.

A glimmer of recognition flashed in Calhoun's eyes. "He's a despicable man. He's on the list of Chace's open cases. I came here to suggest looking into him, as well as Harvey Frank."

"Who's Harvey Frank?" Dylan asked.

"Smalltime trafficker. A little of this little of that. My money is on Duke. I remember Chace saying something about a veiled threat by one of Duke's people if he didn't drop the investigation. This kind of thing happens all the time. Neither Chace nor I gave it much thought."

"What about weapons? This Duke ever transport weapons?" Dylan asked.

"I don't know. I'd have to get into Chace's files. See exactly what he had on him. Chace never really discussed open cases."

"Do you think Duke could be working with anybody inside the department?" Dylan asked.

Calhoun shrugged. "A few days ago, I would have said *no way in hell*. Today, I think anything is possible."

"What changed your mind?" Max asked. "Why did you decide to come here?"

"Reese has me shut out of the case. Says I'm too close emotionally. He won't let me see anything. But since you've been released, there hasn't been any movement. I just want to make sure this gets followed up on and that this case is pursued to its ultimate conclusion."

"Is there anyway we can bring this Duke in for questioning?" Dylan asked.

18

"Press charges against the guys who attacked you. I can pick them up and bring them in for questioning. Maybe we can tie them to Duke," Calhoun said. "We need probable cause in order to bring Duke in himself."

Max rolled her eyes. "Why don't I just beat the information out of them?"

"Let's just do this by the book," Dylan said. "Right now you don't look like you are in the condition to beat the crap out of anybody."

"Don't underestimate me."

"I'll have them picked up," Calhoun said. "I'll let you know as soon as we have them in custody." She ambled for the door, and Dylan saw her out.

Max lay on the couch nursing her wounds. She opened and closed her palm, trying to work on her range of motion. The swelling had already gone down considerably. But she was far from normal.

"I don't know about you, but I'm starving. You want some room service?" Dylan asked.

"Sure. You got a menu?"

Dylan found one on the desk, and brought it over to Max.

She glanced through the offerings and made a selection without much hesitation. "Cheeseburger, sweet potato fries."

Dylan took the menu from her, looked over the selections, then called down to room service.

Max set the glass of ice down on the coffee table, exposing her black eye. "How does it look?"

"Like you got your ass kicked."

"I didn't get my ass kicked." She sneered at him.

"It's better than it was. I still think you should let me take you down to medical."

"I've had worse. Believe me."

There was a moment of silence between them.

"You never really did say what it was like to die?"

"To tell you the truth, I don't remember much. It was like taking a dreamless nap. I was only gone for a few minutes before they revived me. So, probably not long enough to make the journey to the other side. At least, that's what I keep telling myself."

"Why?"

"Because the thought of going to sleep and never waking up terrifies me."

"I think it terrifies us all."

"Yeah, but you weren't born in a test tube."

"What does that have to do with anything?"

Max shrugged. "I don't know. When does a person get a soul? Are they handed out at birth? What if you were never *born*?"

"I don't know. If you're conscious and self-aware, you have a soul."

"What about robots?"

"No. They're machines." Dylan didn't even hesitate with his response.

"What about synthetic people?"

"That's different."

"How?"

Dylan didn't have an answer.

"I'm a biosynthetic organism created in a lab. How is that any different from a robot?"

Dylan shrugged. "I don't know. It's just different."

Max had a sullen look on her face. Contemplating the nature of her own existence was getting to be a routine occurrence for her. Wondering what was beyond, or if there was a beyond, entered her mind more often than she cared to think about. "Sorry. Didn't mean to get all philosophical."

"I don't mind getting philosophical." Dylan smiled.

Max flashed a grim smile back at him.

"What if there is a way to reverse the termination date?"

"If there is, it probably died with Doctor Tor," Max said.

"Then why the urgency to find Silas Rage? He's going to die anyway."

"Because I want the personal satisfaction of killing him myself." Max's eyes had a wicked glint.

"Fair enough."

Room service delivered the food, and they gobbled down their meals. Max leaned back on the couch, stuffed. "You mind if I crash here. I'll regenerate faster if I get some sleep."

"Why don't you take the bedroom? I'll take the couch."

"Really, the couch is fine."

"Take the bedroom. You can lock the door if it makes you feel better. Hell, I'll spring for another suite if you want."

"I'm not worried about you. I can handle you."

"I have no doubt about that."

Max pulled herself off the couch and staggered into the bedroom. "Wake me up when you hear from Calhoun."

Dylan nodded.

Max closed the door behind her and moved into the master bathroom. It was first time she had taken a look at herself since the beating. The swelling was starting to go down, but her face was a train wreck.

On the counter there were complementary packages of soap, shampoo, conditioner, and several sticks of cleansing gum. She popped a stick into her mouth and chewed it for a few moments. The gum lathered up and coated her teeth with nanites that scoured the enamel. It left her teeth clean and minty fresh. She spit the gum in the trashcan, then rinsed her mouth.

Her luggage was probably halfway across the galaxy by now—still aboard the original transport. She was going to have to live on the single serving toiletries until she could either track down her luggage, or buy new stuff. It wasn't that big of a deal—Max liked to travel light anyway.

She peeled out of her clothes and hopped into the shower. Steam filled the room, and the warm water danced on her skin, soothing her sore muscles. She took a *Hollywood* shower, staying in long enough to drain the entire station of hot water.

She toweled off, grabbed a plush robe and slipped

into bed. Now *this* was pillowy soft luxury! A far cry from the prison pod. With any luck, she might actually get some sleep.

Her body melted into the cushiony mattress, her muscles relaxed, and her mind began to let go. The speckled stars of the cosmos flickered through the window—a million pinpoints of light. She was drifting off to somewhere far away when Dylan knocked on the door. The wrapping sounded like thunder, startling her. Max's eyes snapped wide open and her face tensed. "What is it?" She asked, clearly annoyed.

"Sorry to bother you, but I've got a little bit of bad news."

19

"**A**re these the men that attacked you?" Calhoun asked.

Max nodded as she surveyed the corpses of the four men. They were all in cryogenic body bags that had yet to be zipped up and cooled. The men were laid out on hover-gurneys in the incinerator compartment. The massive amount of trash generated by Orion Station was burned to ash, then jettisoned into space. It was part of the new Federation regulations to combat the space junk epidemic. There was nothing worse than hitting heavy space junk at sub-light speed. Hull ruptures from debris impacts used to be unheard of—now they were an accepted risk of high-speed space travel.

Sweat beaded on Max's cheeks from the massive heat generated by the incinerators. The sweltering air reminded her of the unforgiving desert on Thantos 6. The compartment was grimy and soot covered. Rows of trash bins awaited destruction. The pungent smell of rotten waste in the heated environment was enough to make your nose hairs curl and your stomach rumble.

An officer was interviewing the incinerator tech. His face and uniform was smudged black, like he'd been working in a coal mine. Max wondered how he tolerated this horrid environment day in and day out. It was a job that robots could have easily done, but the *Intergalactic Sanitation Workers Union* had kept them out.

"The bodies were dumped in a bin that was headed for the trash incinerator," Calhoun said. "A sanitation employee found them. Each had multiple plasma wounds."

Dylan's face was bathed in concern.

"Any idea who killed them?" Calhoun asked the question pointedly to Max.

Max's eyes narrowed, displeased with Calhoun's accusatory tone. "You're not considering me as a suspect, are you?"

"I can certainly vouch for her whereabouts," Dylan said.

Calhoun arched a curious eyebrow at him. Dylan didn't mean to imply any intimacy with his response, but Calhoun inferred as much. Or, at least, she suspected.

Dylan could almost see the thoughts racing through Calhoun's mind and felt he needed to clarify. "I slept on the couch. Max took the bedroom."

"You're both adults," Calhoun muttered. "What you do is your business."

Max cleared her throat. "There's been no… *doing*."

It was clear the two found each other attractive. Dylan's eyes would casually linger on Max's seductive form at every opportunity. He'd have to be blind not to look. Max had a certain gravity about her that drew men in. And Max would be lying if she said she didn't find Dylan easy on the eyes.

Calhoun shrugged, amused by their protests. "Like I said, that's none of my business."

Detective Reese stormed toward them. He didn't look pleased. "What the hell is she doing here?"

"Identifying bodies," Calhoun said.

"As far as I'm concerned, this is still an active crime scene," Reese barked. "I don't want these two anywhere near here."

Calhoun scowled at him. "I don't see you drumming up any new leads on the case."

Reese's eyes narrowed at her.

"We could use the extra resources," Calhoun said. "All four of these perps have connections to Joe Duke. Chace had been investigating Duke for the last few months. All we need is probable cause to bring him in. These men were our only connection."

Reese sighed. "Do you really think there's something there?"

"It's the best we've got to go on right now," Calhoun said.

Reese was silent a moment as he contemplated the situation. His eyes flicked from Calhoun to Dylan, then to Max, then back to Calhoun. He grabbed her by the arm and pulled her aside, then whispered in her ear. "Alright. If I recall correctly, one of the perps was still alive when you arrived…"

"No," Calhoun said. "They were all dead. They'd been dead for hours."

Reese cleared his throat. "As I was saying, one of the perps was still alive when you arrived, and he confessed to you his involvement in a weapons trafficking scheme with Joe Duke. Is that correct?"

Calhoun stammered. "Uh, yes. I recall something to that effect."

"Excellent. That gives me reasonable suspicion to believe there's a crime in progress on Joe Duke's property. I'll have Judge Abernathy approve a warrant based on your suspicion. We might not be able to get him for murder, but let's see if we can get something to stick on him."

Calhoun nodded.

Reese glanced back over to Max and Dylan. "And those two are your responsibility. They screw anything up, it's your ass."

"Yes, sir."

Max's sensitive hearing allowed her to hear their entire conversation. "So, that's how it's done around here?"

"Do you want to bring Joe Duke in or not?" Calhoun asked.

Max glanced to Dylan. This wasn't exactly by the book. But Dylan was going to let this one slide. "I want to get the man responsible for my brother's murder."

"So do I," Calhoun said.

The coroner sealed the body bags and activated the cryo-systems. He and his assistants pushed them out of the incinerator room and down the corridor, heading to the morgue.

It didn't take long for the warrant to get issued. A tactical team prepared to raid Duke's warehouse. He ran a shipping company as a front, and had built a small empire from his legitimate earnings. His drug trafficking and other illicit activities had boosted his wealth into the stratosphere. Almost everything that was imported into the station touched Joe Duke's hands at one point or another. Either they were coming in on his ships, unloaded by his dockworkers, or stored in his warehouses. It made him almost impossible to catch. If drugs or illicit contraband were found on one of his transport ships, the cargo containers were always registered to a third party. *Duke Shipping* was merely transporting client goods. Contraband housed in one of his warehouses and registered to a client couldn't ever be connected to Duke himself. Though, no one ever seemed to be able to find these mysterious *clients*.

Several OPD officers in black battle armor positioned themselves in the corridor outside the main entrance to Duke's warehouse. It was located in the industrial section of the station. The corridors were wider to accommodate lift equipment and other heavy machinery. There was an entry hatch to the warehouse, along with several large bays.

Max and Dylan positioned themselves near Calhoun and Reese.

"You two, stay outside until the area is secured," Reese said. "The last thing I need is for a Federation agent to get killed, or a civilian to shoot someone."

Max's face tensed. She didn't like sitting on the sidelines.

With the officers in position, Reese tapped his earbud. "Prepare to breach on my command."

20

Amber sparks showered as the plasma torch cut through the hatch. The crackling beam cut the thick steel like cake, dripping beads of molten slag. Once the large rectangular cutout was complete, a battering ram hammered into it, severing the remaining connections, slamming the thunderous plate of steel to the deck.

The tactical squad stormed the compartment with force and precision.

"OPD. We have a warrant. Nobody move!" The squad leader yelled.

It didn't take long before shots were fired. Plasma bolts streaked through the air in all directions. The compartment filled with smoke, and the air had the sharp smell of ionized plasma particles.

The warehouse was a cavernous storage compartment with rows upon rows of shipping containers stacked high atop one another. There were lift-bots moving and stacking containers. Dozens of Duke's men were scattered about the warehouse armed with high-powered plasma rifles. And they weren't afraid to use them.

The sound of impact blasts and body hits filtered into the corridor. Screams of agony wafted through the hatch—it was clear several officers had been hit.

Max grew impatient as a furious battle raged inside the warehouse. It seemed Joe Duke didn't like his privacy invaded. "Sounds like they could use a few extra hands."

"You two are not to get involved in this," Reese said. "Calhoun, come with me."

Reese advanced to the hatch, taking cover behind the remains of the entryway. Calhoun was right behind him. Reese swung the barrel of his plasma pistol around the corner and peered into the warehouse. His eyes widened at the chaos. There were several officers down. The rest of the squad had taken cover behind large cargo containers, exchanging fire with Duke's men at the far end of the warehouse. They were getting pelted from all angles. Some of Duke's men were atop a 2nd level platform, firing down at the officers. Others were situated on catwalks near the roof, sniping at the tactical squad.

The low ground was not the place to be.

Calhoun positioned herself opposite Reese on the other side of the hatch. The two fired off several shots at various targets.

Officer McPherson was writhing on the deck, screeching in pain. He had taken a hit to the abdomen, but was still alive. Plasma blasts impacted the deck around him, sending showers of metal and debris into the air. Plumes of smoke wafted from the blast craters. He was a sitting duck in that position. It was only a matter of time before the sniper on the catwalk scored a direct hit.

Dylan and Max advanced to the entryway.

"I told you to stay put," Reese grumbled.

"You need backup," Max said. "This thing is going south quick."

Several blasts impacted the portal frame. Reese recoiled, then angled his weapon back around and fired several shots at the attacker.

McPherson's screams filled the air.

Reese had a scowl on his face. Enough of this bullshit. He was going to get McPherson out of there. Reese lurched to his feet and raced across the clearing. Plasma bolts zipped in front and behind of him, narrowly missing.

Max laid down a steady stream of suppressive fire at the sniper in the rafters, trying to take some of the focus off Reese as he made his gallant journey.

He reached down, grabbed McPherson's collar and dragged him to safety behind a cargo container. McPherson might not survive the wound, but out of the line of fire, he had a fighting chance.

It was a surprisingly selfless act for a guy like Reese, Max thought. He hadn't impressed her as much of a hero.

The goon on the catwalk plummeted down, tumbling end over end—the result of one of Max's precise plasma bolts. His upper torso caught the edge of a shipping container that was stacked 30 feet in the air, causing the body to spiral like a rag-doll. The impact instantly snapped his spine, and the crack echoed throughout the warehouse like a cannon. His body smacked the deck with a wet slap. Blood oozed from his carcass. So much for staying out of it. It was official now, Max had killed someone on Orion Station. But there was no doubt this guy deserved it. Reese owed Max his life, but she was sure he wouldn't acknowledge the fact.

A flurry of plasma bolts impacted around Max's position. She ducked behind the bulkhead for cover.

Most people couldn't hit the broad side of a star destroyer with a plasma pistol at a distance beyond 50 yards. But Max was dead on accurate. She angled her weapon around the entryway and fired several shots down the narrow corridor between the shipping containers, eviscerating one of Duke's goons. He was barely poking his head out from behind a container when Max's plasma projectile vaporized his skull.

Max pushed into the fray, sprinting for cover behind a cargo container. Plasma bolts erupted at her feet. She scavenged a rifle and a few smoke grenades from the body of a fallen officer. She holstered her pistol and press checked the rifle. She grabbed an extra magazine, then sprang to her feet and raced through the aisles to the port-side bulkhead.

She cautiously advanced forward, toward the far bulkhead, attempting to flank Duke's men. She paused at each aisle, making sure it was clear before she sprinted across to the next.

Plasma bolts from atop one of the containers rained down on her. Max dodged the blazing projectiles and sprinted to the next aisle. She angled her weapon high, firing two rounds. The glowing projectiles clipped the thug, knocking him from atop the container. He crashed to the deck. His elbow shattered on impact.

The goon cried out in agony, writhing on the deck.

He fumbled for his weapon and took aim at Max. But a few well-placed shots put a nice hole in his chest. He wasn't in pain any longer.

Max continued down the narrow corridor, reaching the far bulkhead. She held up at the last row of containers. A staircase led to a second floor loft that housed the office. There was a goon atop the landing with a high-powered plasma rifle, sniping at the OPD officers.

Max lined him up in her sights, and her fingers squeezed the trigger. A bolt rocketed across the compartment. The thug dropped his weapon and fell forward, tumbling over the railing, smacking the deck below.

That drew the attention of several more goons who were at various locations in the loft, defending the office. A flurry of plasma bolts streaked in Max's direction.

Max ducked behind a cargo container as the brilliant bolts erupted all around her. One of them pierced the corner of the container, blasting clear through the material and exiting inches from Max's shoulder. She could feel the searing heat from the energy blast.

If Duke was anywhere in this warehouse, it was going to be in the relative safety of his office. To bring him in, Max was going to have to get past his goons on the second level. But getting up the stairs was going to be a challenge. It was wide open and exposed. She'd be an easy target.

21

P lasma bolts streaked at Max. She was taking fire from multiple positions on the second level, as well as taking fire from down the aisle. She lobbed a smoke canister down the aisle and tossed another one onto the second deck. They both exploded in rapid succession one after the other.

Thunk.

Thunk.

White smoke billowed out, filling the compartment with a milky haze. It was impossible to see anything. Plasma bolts sliced through the fog haphazardly.

Max ran for the stairs. Plasma projectiles whizzed past her. Luck would be the determining factor if she survived. Max activated the thermal imaging in her tactical contact lenses. It allowed her to visualize her opponents through the haze. She unleashed a torrent of weapons fire at the goon squad, peppering them with blistering bolts of energy. She had machine-like precision. Within the span of a few seconds, all of Duke's men protecting the office were flat on the deck.

Max crept toward the office entrance.

A plasma bolt sliced through the thick fog. One of the downed goons still had some life in him and had managed to squeeze off a round. It slammed into Max's weapon, splintering it into blistering hot shards of metal and composite material. The impact knocked the weapon from her hand, and the twisted metal remains clattered across the deck. Max jerked her hand away, stinging from the heat and the force of the impact. Tiny pieces of scalding debris pelted her in the face. She slammed her eyelids shut and recoiled, trying to protect herself. Small bits of metal bore into her skin, searing her flesh.

Max clenched her jaw, flush with the spike of pain. Adrenaline surged, and her pulse pounded in her ears. She was able to stifle the agony and put it in that special place. She was furious. Another flurry of plasma bolts streaked toward her from the downed thug.

Max dove to the deck, tumbling out of the way. She looked like an Olympic gymnast doing a floor exercise, evading the glowing bolts of plasma zipping all around her. She moved with grace and perfection across the deck, somersaulting over the body of another goon, snatching his weapon in the process. In a fluid motion she returned fire, finishing off her assailant. His body went limp, and the plasma bolts stopped flowing in her direction.

Max was pissed. Her face was still bruised and sore from the night before. She hadn't fully healed yet, despite her advanced regenerative capability. The bones in her hand ached, though the swelling had mostly gone down. But now she had bits of metal in her cheek, and she was going to have to pick them out one by one later. Streaks of blood trickled down her face. All that time she spent doing her makeup this morning gone to shit. Falsely accused, beat up, and shot at. She was definitely going to make Joe Duke pay for all of this.

Max stormed toward the office and unleashed a torrent of plasma blasts at the hatch. But they seemed to have little effect, except for some minor pitting and carbon scoring. Joe Duke's office was armor plated. It was going to take more than a plasma rifle to penetrate the composite materials.

The rest of the OPD tactical squad advanced and met Max at the office.

Reese gave her a sharp look. "So much for staying in the rear."

"You weren't making progress. Somebody had to do something."

Reese frowned, but he knew he couldn't argue. "Somebody, cut through this hatch!"

One of the officers put a plasma torch to the composite material, but it wasn't cutting through. Much to his dismay, the material heated to a glowing red, then faded the instant the plasma torch moved away. Within a few seconds, it was cool to the touch. "This thing is thermally shielded, sir. We're not cutting through it. At least, not with this."

The hatch was made out of the same material as re-entry tiles on spacecraft. It was going to take a hell of a lot more than a handheld plasma torch to burn through.

Reese's face tensed, and he marched toward the hatch. He banged on it a few times. "Listen up, Duke. I know you're in there, and we're coming through this hatch, one way or another. Why don't you do us all a favor and open up. I can't be responsible for what happens to you if we have to bust through this damn thing. Tensions are high and trigger fingers are itchy."

There was no response.

A few moments later, a voice called back through the hatch. "Duke says he'll come out on one condition."

"I don't think you're in any position to negotiate," Reese said.

"You think your bogus warrant is going to hold up in court?"

"I think Judge Abernathy will stand behind his warrant."

There was a long silence.

"What's the condition?" Reese asked.

"You grant Duke full immunity from prosecution."

Reese laughed his ass off. "That's a good one. You should write jokes for a living."

There was another long silence.

"You can't stay in there forever, Reese said. "And I'm not going anywhere. You can't wait me out."

"Immunity," the voice said.

"Looks like we're gonna do this the hard way." Reese backed away from the door, and addressed the tactical officers. "Get me a technical bot. Let's see if we can bypass this door."

The officer called headquarters and requested a tech bot. In the meantime, Reese pulled out a pack of cigarettes from his pocket, slid one out, put the filter between his lips, and pulled the cigarette from the pack. He fumbled through his pockets for a laser lighter. He clicked it a few times but he couldn't get it to strike up. He aimed his plasma pistol at one of the corpses of Duke's thugs and blasted off a round. Then he pressed the smoldering barrel to the cigarette. The heat from the barrel turned the tobacco a glowing orange. The cherry lit up as Reese took a deep drag. He filled his lungs, and a wave of soothing calm washed over his face. He exhaled a thick cloud of smoke into the already hazy atmosphere.

"Those things will kill you, you know?" Max said.

"In this line of work? I'm dead long before this thing gets me."

It was an antiquated habit, but some people still couldn't kick it. Reese wasn't about to let his coffee, or his cigarettes, go. They were two things that got him through the tedious day. There were plenty of medical advancements that could combat cancer. But sometimes, some people still just got unlucky.

Reese's mobile rang. The vibration buzzed his pocket. He pulled the thin piece of smart glass out, swiped the display, and held it to his ear. "This is Detective Reese."

"This is Edward R. Maybach. Mr. Duke's attorney. Looking over the warrant, I've noticed an error."

The momentary calm that occupied Reese's face vanished, and the muscles in his jaw began to tense once again. "What kind of error?"

22

"I'm sorry, but Duke is not getting off on a technicality," Reese said.

"I'm afraid he is," Mr. Maybach said. "It appears that whoever filled out the warrant put the wrong date. It's not valid until tomorrow. I suggest you and your people leave the premises immediately."

"Not going to happen. If you think you can invalidate the warrant, you'll have to go through the court system. In the meantime, your client is spending the night in jail."

"That is only making the situation worse for you. As it stands, you are looking at several wrongful death suits. My client tells me your tactical team has taken out at least 10 of his men. When the dust settles on this little incident, if you are not behind bars yourself, you will certainly be looking for a new job."

Reese's face flushed red, and the veins in his neck bulged. "Well, in the meantime I'm still in charge, and I'm gonna take your scumbag client in. So, you can either tell him to come out peacefully, or we will break through. And with tensions as high as they are, I think it's best for your client if he comes out peacefully."

"Is that a threat?"

"I'm just trying to ensure the safety of everyone involved."

"I'll speak with my client." Maybach hung up.

The tech bots showed up and began working on overriding the locking mechanism. But a voice inside the office called through the hatch, "Okay. We're coming out. Don't shoot."

Reese motioned to the tech bots to step away from the hatch. What remained of the tactical squad kept their weapons in the firing position, ready to incinerate Duke and his comrade at the slightest provocation.

The locking mechanism unlatched, and the hatch slid open. Duke's associate stood in the portal with his hands in the air. He was a scruffy guy that hadn't shaved in a few days, and had shaggy brown hair. He was wearing a Hawaiian T-shirt with a white tank top underneath. He had this retro vibe going on, cultivating a 300-year-old clothing style.

Reese's face crinkled up. He hated these retro-chic wannabes. "Come out slowly. Keep your hands where I can see'em."

The man moved slowly, keeping a wary eye on the tactical squad.

"Turn around and place your hands against the bulkhead!"

The man complied, and an officer quickly cuffed him.

Duke sat behind a desk in his office, smoking a cigar. He looked as cool as a cucumber. He wore a finely tailored Zangari suit. The couture garment was hand-crafted, made from rare fibers sourced from Theta Reticuli. It cost more than Reese made in a year. Duke had stark white hair and a square jaw. He had seen just about everything the galaxy had to offer, and nothing fazed him.

Duke took another puff on his cigar, and the cherry glowed red.

Reese leaned in and whispered to Dylan. "I'd like have a few words with him in private before we officially book him. See what I can get out of him. I have a feeling that lawyer of his is going to cut our interview short as soon as we get down to the station."

Dylan shrugged. "It's your show."

Reese stepped into the office. A tactical officer followed behind him and closed the hatch. What was going to happen in there was anyone's guess.

"No, don't get up," Reese said to Duke as he stepped into the office. "Stay seated. I just want to talk for a few minutes before I take you in."

"Have a seat," Duke replied. "Make yourself at home."

Reese took a seat in the chair across the desk from Duke. The tactical officer stayed at the hatch and kept his rifled aimed over Reese's shoulder at Duke.

"Can I offer you a cigar?" Duke asked. "They're all the way from Revnava."

"No, thank you."

The two men stared at each other for a moment—Duke with his hands still in the air. "You boys really fucked this one up, didn't you?"

"Keep your mouth shut, unless I ask you a question," Reese said.

"Whatever you say, Boss." Duke had a cocksure grin.

He just knew he was going to walk away from this whole thing without so much as a citation. And that fact was eating at Reese.

"Lets talk about Chace Carter."

"Who?"

"Don't play games with me."

"I want my attorney present during questioning."

"We're just talking. I haven't arrested you yet."

"Go ahead. Cuff me. Bring me in. We both know I'm going to walk. If you're not going to arrest me, I suggest you fuck off and get out of here."

"I suppose you have a pistol in one of those desk drawers?"

Duke nodded.

"Why don't you show it to me?"

"You're welcome to look for yourself." Duke smiled. He wasn't going to play Reese's game.

"Do me a favor," Reese asked. "Place your palms atop the desk. Slowly."

Duke's eyes narrowed at him, skeptically. But he complied. "When I think about all the inept, incompetent police officers, you are always at the top of my list, Detective."

"Thank you. I'm flattered."

"You have no idea just how bad you've fucked yourself."

"We'll see, won't we?"

Reese set his pistol on the desk in between Duke's hands. He spun the grip around to face Duke. All it would take was a millisecond and the weapon would be in Duke's palm. Another fraction of a second to pull the trigger, and Reese would be dead.

Duke's eyes flicked to the pistol, then back to Reese.

His eyes surveyed the tactical officer by the hatch—the barrel of his weapon staring Duke in the face. "Do you really think I'm that fucking stupid?"

"I don't know, you look pretty stupid to me."

The muscles in Duke's jaw twitched. But he didn't make a move for the pistol. Under normal circumstances, Duke wouldn't suffer insults. So much as a sideways glance could get you killed.

"You know, that was a real shame about Eddie."

At the mere mention of his name, Duke's face tightened even further.

"He was such a young kid. Had a full life ahead of him. It was really tragic what happened."

"You think you can get me all riled up talking about my little brother?"

"I'm not trying to get you riled up. I didn't realize it was such a touchy subject for you." Reese knew damn good and well how touchy it was.

Duke said nothing.

"I bet you'd like to get your hands on the guy who killed Eddie, wouldn't you?"

"I get my hands on the guy who killed Eddie, then you'll have something to arrest me for."

"That's good." Reese leaned in and whispered across the desk, "Because you're looking at him."

23

D uke's face boiled with rage. The veins in his forehead bulged. It was easy to see that he wanted to grab the pistol and rattle off several shots into Reese. But Duke didn't get to be a criminal overlord without willpower and discipline. If Duke so much as flinched, the officer by the hatch would blast a hole in his head.

"You know what I think?" Duke said. "I think you're full of shit. I think you're making up a story so I'll go for the gun, then you've got an excuse to shoot."

"I wouldn't make up a story about something like that. I just feel like you deserve to know the truth," Reese said with mock sincerity. "You need to know the intimate details of how he died. Because it wasn't quick. I must have beaten him for hours, trying to get information out of him. But you'd be proud to know, he wouldn't talk."

Duke was getting so angry that he began to sweat. Small beads of perspiration formed on his forehead and cheeks. His lip twitched, and his hands developed a small tremor as he fought the urge to take action.

"I've found that one of the most effective interrogation techniques is the simplest. I just take a hammer and smash it against a person's fingernail as hard as I can. It's excruciating. It's not life-threatening, but it throbs and aches with unbearable pain. Research shows that the fingertips are one of the most sensitive areas of the human body. I've found that if you inflict that kind of pain right up front, people start wondering how much worse it's going to get. Your imagination runs wild and you envision all kinds of horrid scenarios. I mean, *this was just fingertips, what happens when this guy works his way to my eyes? What happens when he cracks my kneecaps? How much worse is it going to get?*"

Duke looked like he was about to explode.

"You know I got through all 10 of his fingers and he didn't say a word. You should have seen him. He was crying and begging for me to stop. I almost felt sorry for him. *Almost.* But that didn't keep me from breaking both of his kneecaps. I've never seen anybody take that much pain. But after all that, not a word. So what was I going to do? I couldn't bring him down to the station and arrest him in that condition. These kinds of torture tactics are illegal. I couldn't just let him go. He might have filed charges against me. That would have been a bad career move. So I had to put him in an airlock and spaced him. You know what happens to the body when exposed to the vacuum of space? Don't worry. That was probably the least painful part of the whole ordeal. And it didn't last long."

Duke's eyes blazed into Reese.

"You know, I think about him often. Every time I

look out there at the cosmos I think of Eddie drifting along for all eternity among the flickering stars. If he would have given up information about you, I would have let him go."

Duke's eyes brimmed, partly from sadness, partly from anger. His lips snarled like an angry beast—he was a wolf poised to leap across the desk and rip Reese's throat out with his teeth.

For an instant, Reese thought Duke was going to crack and reach for the gun. But the ruthless criminal took a deep breath and composed himself.

"You're lying."

"Am I?" Now it was Reese that had the cocksure grin. He dug into his pocket and pulled out a ring. He tossed it onto the desk. It spun a few times before it came to a stop.

Duke's eyes flared at the site. He recognized the ring all too well. It was Eddie's. Duke had one just like it that he wore on his pinky finger. It was a symbol of their unbreakable brotherhood. Duke glanced from Eddie's ring to his own. Duke clenched his jaw, the boiling rage under his reddened face about to erupt. This was the tipping point.

Duked lunged for the pistol, but before he could get a shot off, the officer by the hatch put two blistering plasma bolts into Duke—one in his chest, and one in his head.

Duke's body fell back against the chair.

"Well, my work here is done," Reese said, pleased with himself. He grabbed his pistol that had fallen from Duke's hands. He holstered it, then winked at the tactical officer. "Self-defense. It had to be done."

24

"You people are absolute morons," the man in the Hawaiian shirt exclaimed. He was livid. He paced around Reese's office without restraints. "I've been working undercover for over a year and a half. I finally get close to Duke, and you guys come in and pull this shit."

"Sorry," Reese said without any trace of sincerity. He sat behind his desk, feet up like he didn't have a care in the world.

"Next week a shipment of hervoxin is coming in, and I was supposed to meet with the supplier. We've never been able to discover Duke's source. And I was this close," he gestured with his thumb and index finger. Agent Prescott was with the Drug Enforcement Agency." I guess it didn't occur to anyone to check with us before instigating a raid on one of the largest narcotic traffickers in the area?"

"I guess it didn't occur to your agency to inform us you were engaged in an undercover operation in our jurisdiction?" Reese countered.

Prescott grumbled to himself. Then, looking to shift the blame, pointed his finger at Max. "And this one... She damn near killed everyone in that warehouse. Is she even a cop?"

Reese fumbled for words. "She's part of a special task force on... crime. Recently deputized."

Prescott's eyes blazed into Max. She forced a smile and went along with it. It was quite a surprise that Reese was defending her, but his ass was on the line now.

"We identified ourselves as police officers before the raid," Reese said. "They responded with weapons fire. As far as I'm concerned, they were all clean kills."

Prescott shook his head, not buying it for a second. "And what's the DA going to say about it when Duke's attorney presses for an investigation?"

"The mayor is determined to clean up the station. I think the DA will see our actions in line with the mayor's initiative. He wants us to be a center for intergalactic commerce."

Prescott scoffed. "Mayor's initiative?" he said mockingly. "Orion Station is a center for intergalactic crime. Always has been, always will be." He paused a moment. "You should have never been alone in the office with Duke. If you'd have just left him alive, the deal next week might still have gone through. Instead, we lost one of the largest narcotics traffickers in the galaxy."

"I wasn't alone with Duke," Reese snapped. "Officer Tidwell was with me. He can verify that Duke reached for my weapon. He had no choice but to take the suspect out."

Dylan interjected. "Unfortunately, this case is no closer to solving my brother's murder."

"I can assure you, the perpetrator of the crime has been brought to justice," Reese said.

"We'll never really know for sure now, will we?" Dylan said.

"I've got thousands of hours of recorded conversations between Duke and his associates," Prescott said. "What information are you looking for?"

"We're trying to determine Duke's involvement in the death of Detective Chace Carter," Dylan said.

Agent Prescott pulled out his mobile device. He tabbed through a few screens and launched an app. All of the surveillance audio and video Prescott had collected had been transcribed and indexed upon import into the application. The contents of the files were keyword searchable. Prescott was able to plug in the name Chace Carter, and within moments, a list of files that contained the name were displayed on the screen. Prescott scrubbed through them one by one, listening to the sections surrounding the utterance of Chace's name. It didn't take long to undercover a conversation of interest. An angry voice boomed through the speaker on Prescott's mobile device as he replayed a file. "I want that son-of-a-bitch dead. I don't care how it gets done. Just do it." There was no doubt the voice belonged to Duke.

"He's a cop. Don't you think that might bring down a little heat?" another man responded.

Prescott stopped the playback. "The second voice you hear is Tom Corrigan." He pressed play again.

"I know who he is," Duke grumbled. "And it's not going to bring anything down on me if you do it correctly. If you can't do it, I'll move on it. And that's the last thing you want me to do. Because in that scenario, what do I need you for? I only keep people around me who are useful. Are you useful?"

"Yes, sir."

"Good. Agent Carter's death needs to look like an accident. If you can't make it look like an accident, you need to set someone up to take the fall. Either way, if Carter is still breathing by the end of the week, you're not going to be. Have I made myself clear?"

"Yes, sir," the associate stammered.

Prescott stopped the playback. "It doesn't necessarily prove Duke had Carter killed. But he's at least guilty of conspiracy to commit murder. I'd say Corrigan is the shooter."

"Where is Corrigan now?" Dylan asked. "Can we bring him in for questioning?"

"You could, but he ain't going to say much," Prescott said.

"Why not?"

"Cause dead in the warehouse."

Reese smiled. "All's well that ends well."

Dylan was still skeptical. But it was probably the closest thing to closure that he was going to get.

25

"I guess that's it," Max said.

Dylan shrugged. "I guess."

Max could sense his doubt. She poured herself a drink from the minibar in Dylan's suite. She moved in front of the mirror and started picking the pieces of shrapnel out of her face. She winced as she removed each tiny shard. She gazed at her complexion and frowned. There was still a dark circle under her eye from the day before, now this. It would take a few days to heal, and even then she might need skin resurfacing.

"You got any antibiotic cream?"

"Do you have some kind of aversion to doctors?"

"Yes."

Dylan dug into his suitcase, pulled out a gel tube, and tossed it to Max. She disappeared into the bathroom and pulled the rest of the tiny shards from her skin. She washed the blood from her face and applied the antibiotic cream. She glanced in the mirror, adjusted her hair and shrugged. This was as good as it was going to get for now. She took a sip of her drink and strolled back into the living room.

"Where are you going to go now?" Dylan asked.

"Well, first thing I'm going to do is track down my luggage. I had some really cute outfits in my bag. But I'm sure they're halfway across the galaxy by now."

Dylan chuckled. "Somehow I think you could make any outfit look cute."

"Flattery will get you everywhere, Mr. Carter." Her crystal blue eyes sparkled at him. "What about you?"

"I guess I'm heading back to headquarters." He paused for a moment, then pulled out his mobile device. He tabbed through a few screens. "I'm sending you all the information I have on Silas Rage. It would be's remiss of me if I didn't suggest you let sleeping dogs lie, but since I know you're not going to do that, good luck." Dylan hesitated a moment. "If you ever find yourself on Cygnus Minor 3, look me up."

Max's sultry eyes flicked to Dylan. A slight grin curled on her lips. "I just might do that."

There was a little something between them, but neither one knew what the hell it was. Dylan's mobile rang, interrupting whatever moment was brewing. It was Agent Prescott.

"I did some checking. Tom Corrigan wasn't the shooter. He wasn't aboard the station at the time of the murder."

"Thanks. I appreciate the info."

"Where are you staying?"

"The Plaza."

"I'll swing by in a few hours. I've got something you might be interested in." Prescott ended the call before Dylan had a chance to inquire further.

"What is it? Max asked.

"Looks like our work here isn't done."

Max frowned. She pondered their next move. "Somebody had to see something."

"OPD canvased the area. They talked to all the shop owners and as many store patrons as they could find. No one saw anything."

"And you trust the OPD?"

Dylan's face crinkled up. "You're right. Let's go see what we can find."

Dylan followed Max down to the lobby and out into the maze of corridors, weaving their way to the crime scene. The two hovered outside the men's restroom in the shopping district.

Dylan seemed hesitant. "I don't think I can go in there."

Max glanced at the storefronts nearby. She pointed at the cashier of the *Arkani* men's clothing boutique that was directly across from the restroom. "Unobstructed view of the restroom from the cash register. If anybody saw anything, it would likely be somebody in this store. Why don't you go see what you can find out. I'll check out the restroom."

Dylan arched a single eyebrow at her.

"Don't worry. I can handle myself." She sent Dylan into the boutique, then she pushed into the men's restroom.

There were a couple of guys taking care of business at the urinals while she started searching the compartment for clues. There were still blood stains in grooves between the deck—despite the fact the restroom had been cleaned multiple times since the murder. She didn't know what she was looking for. It was probably just a dead-end anyway. Any shoe prints, or plasma residue, would be long gone.

She got a few sideways glances from the men.

"You looking for something, sweetheart?" A burly guy said, looking over his shoulder from a urinal. "Whatever it is, I can help you find it," he said with a lascivious wink.

"I don't know, seems like what you've got might be pretty hard to find."

The man's grin turned to a scowl. He pulled up his pants and stormed out of the restroom.

Max continued scouring the facility. There was nothing of interest in the bathroom. Only a small crater from where the plasma bolt had exited Chace's skull and pitted the bulkhead above the urinal. It had created a tiny hole through to the women's restroom. She peered through the narrow aperture and could see the other side. From this angle, she could only see women primping in the mirror.

Max pushed back into the corridor and went into the women's restroom. She found the hole from the blast mark. She looked across to the opposite bulkhead to see if the plasma bolt had continued through with any measurable force. She was trying to get an idea of how powerful the killer's weapon was. But the opposite bulkhead didn't seem to be affected.

She gave one last glance around the restroom before heading back into the corridor. Something caught her eye—a black dot on the bulkhead, near the ceiling. She climbed up to reach it. The spot turned out to be a small camera, stuck to the bulkhead. It was the size of a small button, with an adhesive back. She pried it loose, then hopped down. She held the device in her palm, studying it. It was clearly transmitting wirelessly to a nearby receiver. Someone was peeping on the women's restroom.

Max pushed back into the corridor and scanned the area. She caught sight of the station janitor rounding the corner, pushing a cleaning cart.

A slight grin curled up on Max's lips. She strolled to the dumpy guy pushing the cart. "Mind if I ask you a few questions."

The man looked nervous and stammered, "I'm really busy. Behind schedule."

"It will only take a few minutes."

"I got six more restrooms to clean, if I don't finish them by the end of my shift, I'll get docked pay."

Max held out her palm, displaying the camera.

The janitor swallowed hard, and his face went pale. He looked guilty as sin.

Max knew she had her man. She pointed to Dylan who was questioning the store clerk. "You see that guy in there? He's an FCIS agent. I bet he would love to hear about your illegal recording activities. You could go away for a long time for something like this."

26

"Y ou're not going to arrest me, are you?"

"Not if you cooperate," Dylan said.

Max and Dylan interrogated the janitor in a small utility compartment away from public eyes.

"How many cameras do you have placed in restrooms on the station?" Max asked.

The janitor shrugged. "All of them."

"Even the men's rooms?" Max asked.

"No. Just the women's."

"Well, that doesn't really do us any good, does it?" Dylan said.

"You're looking for information about the murder, aren't you?"

"What do you know?" Dylan asked.

"I saw who did it."

Dylan's eyes widened.

"Who?"

"I don't know what her name was. She looked a lot like you," the janitor said, pointing to Max. "Not identical or anything, but same build, same hair color. Good looking."

"Why didn't you say anything before? Report it to the authorities?" Max asked.

"My life may not seem like much, but I don't want to lose it. I learned a long time ago to keep my mouth shut about things I see on the station."

"How did you see the murder?"

"I was in the restroom, taking care of business in one of the stalls. I heard the pistol go off, then looked over the divider to see the dead man on the deck and the girl rushing out of the compartment. It's a good thing she didn't check the stalls, or I'd be dead too."

Dylan and Max exchanged a glance.

"So, we're all good, right? I told you what you want to know, and you guys forget about my creative filmmaking."

"What exactly do you do with this footage? You get off to this?" Max asked.

The janitor's face twisted up. "No. I'm not into that kind of thing. Lady, you don't know the kind of people that are out there on the Galactic net. People pay big money for these clips. And cash is tight. The robots undercut everything, and our union isn't as strong as the sanitation department."

Max looked astonished. "People pay for this?"

"High dollar."

"To watch women pee?"

"It takes all kinds, Lady."

"How much of this stuff do you have?"

"I got at least three years of footage. 24 hours a day, seven days a week. Of course, not all of it is usable."

"Tell you what. I'm going to give you 24 hours to

remove all the cameras from every restroom on this facility. And destroy all the footage."

The janitor's eyes widened. "All the footage?"

"All of it. I'm going to pull a search warrant and have Federation agents search your premises. So you better hurry and get rid of everything."

The janitor grumbled, but what choice did he have? He was getting off easy.

Max and Dylan let the janitor go, then stepped back into the corridor.

"Do you think he's telling the truth?" Max asked.

Dylan shrugged. "I don't know. Seems like people have an aversion to the truth on this station." He sighed, heavy with frustration. "Why don't you run back to the hotel room, I'll meet you there."

"Where are you going?"

"I'm gonna run down a lead—a clerk from the boutique that was working at the time of the murder."

"Want me to go with you?"

"I need you to go back to the hotel and wait for Prescott. He said he's got some information that might help."

Max and Dylan parted ways.

Weaving through the maze of corridors, Max made her way back toward the hotel room. But she had the distinct feeling that she was being followed. She kept glancing over her shoulder, catching sight of a robot weaving in and out of the crowd, trying to keep up.

Max turned the corner at the next junction, then pressed her back flat against the bulkhead and waited. When the robot rounded the corner after her, she grabbed the android and slammed him against the bulkhead. She placed the barrel of her plasma pistol against his head.

The robot's nervous eyes went wide. "My name is Winston. It's urgent that I speak with you."

He was a sleek XR-709 service bot. He stood 5'10" tall with composite plastic body panels, designed by the famed sports car designer Zapharini, over an alloy skeleton. Precision crafted gears, servos, and joints allowed Winston to have smooth and fluid movement. A composite smart-polymer allowed him to form expressions on his face plate. He was state-of-the-art, and one of the more expensive models. *Too* expensive for a cop to afford.

It took Max a moment to realize who Winston was. "You're Chace's personal bot."

"Yes. Is there somewhere more private we could speak? I'm taking a big risk by approaching you."

Max pulled him into a storage compartment adjacent to the main hallway.

"Everyone's been looking for you."

"I know. But it hasn't been safe. And I haven't been sure who I could trust. I have information that I think could be beneficial."

"Regarding Chace's death?"

"Yes."

"Do you know who killed him?"

Winston hesitated for a moment. "Are you familiar with the Crygon Sphere?" Winston asked.

Max nodded. "It's a weapon the size of a baseball that could destroy an entire planet."

"According to my information, there will be several hundred of them at this facility in a few days."

Max's eyes widened. "That's impossible. The materials needed to create those weapons are few and far between. The technology to construct the device is extremely advanced. No one outside the Federation government has been able to create one. And certainly not in that number."

"Perhaps that may have been true in the past. But we are entering a new era of unprecedented terror."

Max processed the information.

"Chace was working on uncovering a massive arms trading network. The information he gathered, which is now stored in my data systems, implicates the highest members of regional government. I believe that is why he was killed."

"And you know who his killer is?"

"That, I believe, I can prove with a reasonable degree of certainty."

27

"Those are pretty bold allegations," Max said. "And you have the evidence to back this up?"

"The evidence I have implicates several members of the OPD, Customs Enforcement Agents, the district attorney, and implicates Mayor Thornton."

"And you're sure about this?"

"Yes. The mayor's own shipping company, *Starway Express*, a subsidiary of *Thornton Enterprises*, is more than likely facilitating transport of the illegal arms shipments."

"Why didn't Chace transmit this information back to the FCIS?"

"Any transmission made from this facility will be intercepted and decrypted by the Orion Station Security Agency," Winston said. "Transmitting the data would have blown Chace's cover. Plus, he also felt unsure about contacts within the FCIS."

Max looked surprised. "You think there is corruption within the FCIS?"

"It is entirely possible that insurgents have infiltrated the agency. Also, do not dismiss the financial incentives for participating in illegal weapons trafficking."

Max took a solemn pause.

"I am the key to bringing the network down. They will do anything to see to my destruction."

"You're safe with me."

"I don't know if even you could protect me. The corruption on Orion Station is systemic."

"Let's get back to the hotel room and wait for Dylan. We'll get you off the station and back to FCIS headquarters," Max said, trying to reassure the worried bot.

The two stepped into the hallway. There was a moderate amount of foot traffic—people coming and going. Max scanned the corridor—no one seemed overtly hostile. But it didn't take long before a flurry of plasma bolts streaked in their direction.

Several goons at the end of the corridor blasted at the two. Glowing plasma bolts sliced the air, eviscerating innocent bystanders. The head of a woman walking next to Max exploded, splattering bits of crimson goo across the bulkheads. Her limp body flopped to the deck. Shrieks of terror filled the narrow corridor. Pedestrians scattered in all directions.

Max ducked for cover and returned fire. "Go, go, go," Max shouted to Winston as she laid down a steady stream of suppressive fire. Winston took off running down the corridor. Max blasted off a few more shots, then sprinted after him. There were too many goons to stand and fight toe-to-toe. Max was outnumbered and outgunned.

Plasma bolts zipped all around her as she raced to

catch up with Winston. They turned the corner at the next junction and sprinted down the hallway.

The goons gave chase, peppering the corridors with a steady onslaught of plasma projectiles. Sparks showered from the bulkheads as projectiles impacted. Pedestrians were sliced by blistering bolts, or mowed down by the thugs as they barreled through the passageways. The goons all wore face shields, obscuring their identities.

Max ran as fast as she could. Her heart was pounding, and her quads were burning. Her chest heaved for breath. She would turn and fire the occasional shot over her shoulder in an attempt to slow the goons down, but they kept coming.

Max was a conditioned athlete. Her superior genetics ensured that. There was no doubt, she was probably one of the fastest runners on the station. But Winston was faster. Winston didn't get tired. His muscles didn't fatigue. He didn't need oxygen. He could maintain this speed until his joints wore out, which, according to the manufacturer, would be sometime after a billion use cycles.

Max and Winston snaked through a few passageways, then sprinted out into the park. It was a lush green oasis with synthetic trees and grass. There was a lake in the center of the park that was home to an array of ducks and other wildlife. A domed skylight provided a stunning view of the cosmos and let in natural light from the nearby star, Delta Centuri.

The park was surrounded on all sides by luxury apartments. It was the only place in the whole station where you could get a balcony that had a natural view and sunshine. And they weren't cheap either. Why anyone would pay that kind of money to live on this facility was beyond Max.

Max and Winston sprinted over the gentle rolling slopes, weaving between the trees. Plasma bolts blasted all around them, impacting the synthetic trees, leaving smoldering craters.

Max angled her weapon back and fired a few shots off, and continued running. She managed to take out one of the goons. His body crashed to the synthetic grass.

People in the park scattered.

Max made her way across the park to the financial district. She sprinted down an avenue, then cut across an alleyway. This section of the station resembled the downtown area of any major metropolitan city, only this city was encased in a dome. The streets were narrow and populated only with pedestrians, hover boards, and personal hover scooters. The transit system was a deck below, and tram cars navigated an interconnected maze of passageways spanning the circumference of the station. It was the fastest way to get from one end of the sprawling complex to the other.

Max twisted and turned through the streets, then plunged down a staircase to the sub-transit system.

Winston followed behind her. "Are you sure this is such a good idea? According to the transit schedule, another tram won't reach the platform for another 96 seconds. We will be in a most vulnerable position."

Max ignored him and sprinted down the steps anyway. Alarms sounded as they ran through the toll-booth without paying. A security bot started after them, but changed his mind as the goons' plasma bolts sliced through the air. The security bot quickly retreated back to the safety of his booth.

The horde of goons raced through the toll scanners, sprinting after Max and Winston.

Just as Winston had predicted, the platform was empty. There wasn't a tram in sight.

Max took cover behind a support pylon and returned fire at the goons. Winston hid behind a pylon as well, making himself as slim as possible.

The crowd waiting for the tram dispersed in screaming panic. A flurry of plasma bolts filled the compartment. Sparks showered from the pylons as plasma projectiles impacted.

Max angled around the barrier and squeezed off a few rounds, then ducked for cover.

The goons had held up near the entrance to the platform, firing from around the corner. A team of them advanced to a near support pylon. Max wasn't going to be able to hold them off forever, and she was almost out of ammunition.

28

Max fired off several more rounds, taking out one of the goons as he attempted to dart from one pylon to the next. His head vaporized in a pink mist, and his body splatted against the platform.

Winston counted the seconds until the tram arrived. As he reached 96, the tram pulled up to the platform and the doors slid open. Unsuspecting passengers began to step off. One lady took a plasma bolt to the chest. She was dead before her high heels hit the platform. She crashed down, shattering the set of crystal inside her shopping bag. She was apparently on her way to return some items to the shopping district.

It didn't take a rocket scientist to figure out this was a bad place to get off the tram. The majority of the passengers cowered in the compartment, praying the doors would close soon and the tram would be on its way.

Max angled around the pylon and unleashed a torrent of plasma projectiles at the goons. But her stream of fire abruptly ended as she ran out of ammo. The magazine was empty. She holstered the pistol, then shouted at Winston to sprint for the tram. The two raced across the platform as plasma bolts zipped all around them.

Max dove into the tram compartment just as the doors slid shut. She looked back at her attackers through the window as they peppered the tram with plasma bolts. But the electromagnetic shielding of the tram kept the projectiles from registering any damage. The projectiles dissipated in a static discharge.

Max flipped off her assailants as the tram began to move away.

In an instant, Max and Winston were zipping through a maze of dark tunnels in the station. Passengers gawked at the odd couple—eyes wide and mouths agape. *Who were these people? And what the hell had just happened?*

Max and Winston took a seat as the other passengers slowly peeled themselves off the ground, trembling with fear.

Max gave Winston a look. "Nice friends you've got there."

"They are not my friends. I warned you that multiple entities seek to destroy me."

"Those guys were a bunch of pussies. If I hadn't run out of ammo, they'd be scraping them off the platform."

"While I can appreciate your confidence, that is not exactly how I recall the situation."

Max chuckled. "We are still alive, aren't we?"

"*You* are alive. I only give off the impression of life due to my anthropomorphic features and artificial intelligence."

"You need to lighten up."

Winston looked confused. "Are you suggesting I acquire more illumination? Or that I should lighten the shade of my body panels?"

"It's a figure of speech. I'm surprised Chace didn't give you a more casual personality profile."

"I have a defective social processing module. I believe it is one of the reasons why Chace was able to afford this model."

"So, he got you at a scratch and dent sale?"

"I am neither scratched, nor dented."

Max laughed. "I'll take a look at your circuits after a while. If you and I are going to spend any length of time together, you're going to need to acquire a sense of humor. Otherwise it's a deal-breaker."

Winston appeared worried. "I would very much like it if we could maintain our friendship."

Max smiled at him. "Don't worry, Winston. I'm not letting you out of my sight."

"That's reassuring."

Max pulled out her mobile device from her pocket and called Dylan, but there was no response. Max and Winston stayed on the tram until they reached a stop near the Plaza.

The two cautiously stepped off the tram and made their way to the lobby. Max wasn't at all comfortable with the fact that she was out of ammunition. And the lobby was full of potential threats.

Max weaved her way through the crowd to the elevator banks. It was an agonizing few moments while she waited for the bell to ring, and the doors to slide open. Max and Winston stepped inside along with a few other passengers. She kept a watchful eye on them.

One by one, they stepped off at various levels without incident. Max breathed a sigh of relief.

She stepped off the elevator with trepidation and made her way down the corridor. But the hatch to Dylan's suite was in shambles. It had been blasted open, having taken heavy fire from a plasma rifle.

"Wait here," Max whispered to Winston.

Max pushed into the suite with caution. She could see from the entrance foyer that the place had been ransacked. She glanced to her side—the kitchen was empty. All the cabinets had been flung open and several dishes were smashed in pieces on the tile. Someone had been searching for something.

Max proceeded down the foyer, into the living area.

The hard barrel of a plasma pistol pressed against her skull—a thug had been waiting around the corner for her.

"Just take it nice and easy," the thug said "Don't do anything stupid."

29

The plasma pistol fired as Max made her move. With lightning speed, she shifted her head aside, dodging the plasma projectile. She simultaneously grabbed the assailant's wrist, pushing the weapon aside. With her other hand, she reached across and grabbed the barrel. She twisted the pistol back, snapping the assailant's finger caught in the trigger guard. She planted a knee in the attacker's groin. He doubled over as she stripped the weapon from his hand. She swung the barrel around and took aim.

But the goon sprang to his feet and tackled Max before she had fully lined him up in her sights. He pinned her to the ground, and the two struggled over the weapon. He slammed her wrist against the ground, and the weapon clattered away, skidding across the deck.

Winston just watched the whole thing. He looked terrified and wasn't about to step in.

Max kicked the thug off of her, and the two scrambled to their feet. They both took defensive postures, sizing each other up.

The goon jabbed twice, then swung a hard right. Max deflected the blow and wrenched his arm around. She slammed her knee into his abdomen. As he doubled over, she finished him off with an elbow to the back of the head. The blow sent him crashing to the ground. He tried to push himself off the floor, but Max put a boot in his rib cage. The snap and crackle of broken bones filled the air.

Max trotted across the room and picked up the pistol.

Her attacker was still groaning on the ground. She moved back toward him and put the pistol against his head. "Who are you working for?"

"Fuck you," the ass-clown said.

Max pistol-whipped him in the back of his head. The blow opened up a juicy gash on his scalp, and blood oozed into his hair.

"We can play this game all day long," Max said. "Who are you working for?"

"You'll find out soon enough."

Max whacked him again."

"Jesus, Lady," he said, grimacing.

"Hurts, doesn't it?"

"Look, I was just sent here to get the robot."

"By whom?"

"Thornton. I work for Thornton."

"Go back to Thornton and tell him I'm coming for him. I don't like it when people try to set me up. And I sure don't like it when people try to kill me."

Max backed away and let the goon get up. "If I see you again, you're a dead man, you got that?"

The goon nodded.

She kept the weapon trained on him as he staggered to his feet. On his way up, he grabbed for a small backup pistol from his ankle holster. The goon should have learned his lesson. He wasn't faster than Max. She could strike like a cobra.

A plasma bolt incinerated his head before he his backup cleared his ankle holster.

The goon's body crumbled to the deck.

"Dumbass," Max muttered to herself. Her eyes afflicted to Winston. "You were a lot of help,"she said, her voice dripping with sarcasm.

"As I'm sure you are aware, it is against my programming to harm a human being—even in self-defense."

"Well, you could have grabbed the gun during the struggle. That wouldn't have harmed anyone."

Winston shrugged. "You seemed to do okay without my help."

Max sneered at him. "Come on. We need to get out of here."

"I agree. I don't feel entirely safe here."

Max stepped into the hallway, and made her way to the elevators. She tossed a few credits onto the supply cart as she passed a cleaning bot. "6302 is a real mess."

"Yes, ma'am," the bot responded, having no idea it would find a dead body waiting. Though, on Orion Station, it wouldn't be unusual.

Max pressed the call button, and waited for the elevator with her pistol aimed at the doors. She wasn't taking any chances.

The elevator dinged, and the occupants screeched in terror as the doors slid open—a plasma pistol staring them in the face wasn't exactly what they expected.

Max lowered her weapon and let the occupants ease off the lift. They hugged the wall as they skirted around her and moved cautiously away.

Max and Winston stepped aboard and hit the lobby button. The door slid shut, and the elevator descended rapidly. It stopped on a lower level and Max kept her weapon aimed at the door.

Horrified hotel guests looked on in terror and instantly raised their hands in the air at the sight of the weapon. It was an elderly couple.

Max felt bad—she had probably almost given them a heart attack. "Sorry. Elevator's full."

The couple slowly nodded and waited for the doors to close. The lift plunged down, and after a few similar incidents, Max and Winston reached the lobby. With crowds of people coming and going, Thornton's goons could have been anywhere.

Max and the robot casually stepped off the elevator and strolled through the lobby. There was a large common area with couches and coffee tables and display screens. There was an office area, a bar, a restaurant, and a coffee shop. The high vaulted ceilings were supported with towering columns. It was elegantly adorned with exquisite decor. There was an old-fashioned black grand piano, and an entertainment bot was sitting before it, playing a beautiful rendition of Mozart's *Piano Concerto 21*. He was joined by a small orchestral accompaniment, each instrument played by a bot with virtuoso skill. They were all dressed in tuxedos, and filled the lobby with beautiful music 24 hours a day, seven days a week. With bots like that, it was impossible for human classical musicians to make a living. They had a skill and breadth of knowledge that was unparalleled. They could play any song from any classical composer upon request. Their renditions were flawless, yet contained all the nuances and passion of the best human performances. All of which were incorporated into their database. If they ever made a mistake, it was on purpose to give the music a more natural feel.

Max kept the pistol at her side, ready to engage any threats. It was smooth sailing at first. But a quarter of the way through the lobby, Max caught sight of something troubling at the entrance. The goons that she had left behind at the sub-transit station had caught up with her.

30

P lasma blasts erupted, filling the lobby with deadly projectiles. Max took cover behind one of the marble pillars. She fired at the masked goons as they stormed into the lobby.

Panicked guests scattered in all directions, screaming and hollering. Hotel employees ducked for cover behind the check-in counter. The robots kept playing Mozart. The concerto echoed off the vaulted ceiling and provided the soundtrack for the shootout.

Plasma blasts peppered the marble pillar Max was hiding behind, sending chips of debris showering out, leaving small craters behind.

Winston took cover behind one of the columns and fidgeted nervously. He was extremely high strung for a robot.

Max angled the barrel of her plasma pistol around the pillar and unleashed a flurry weapons fire. She took out two of the thugs in quick succession, but more spilled into the entryway, stepping over the bodies of their fallen comrades.

Max ducked behind the column, avoiding the stream of plasma projectiles as the goons returned fire. The intense bolts sizzled as they ripped through the air. The lobby filled with haze and the distinct scent of charged particles.

Two of the goons sprinted to the side lounge. They took cover behind a couch. Max knew they were attempting to flank her. She was now taking fire from multiple positions. If the goons advanced laterally any farther, the pillar wasn't going to offer Max much protection.

Max blasted at the thugs cowering behind the couch. Some of her shots impacted the fabric, setting the piece of furniture ablaze. Others zipped over the top, streaking past the orchestral musicians. The robots didn't seem fazed in the least. They kept creating beautiful music, filling the compartment with the glorious concerto.

Max's fervent eyes glanced up to the chandelier in the lounge. It was an old-fashioned antique hanging directly above the goons. Max unleashed a stream of weapons fire at the fixture, severing the chain that held the massive structure. The chandelier crashed down and shattered atop the goons. The crushing weight and brass branches punctured their flesh, oozing a steady flow of blood onto the tile.

Max angled her weapon at the remaining goons posted up at the entryway. She could feel the searing heat of the plasma projectiles as they whizzed past her. With blazing speed, she lined up one of the goons in her sights and squeezed the trigger. Before the projectile had even vaporized his head, she had focused on the next thug. She fired off two quick blasts, then targeted the last of the goons. But he managed to get a quick shot off.

The bolt screamed toward Max.

She ducked behind the pillar, shifting to the other side. She angled her weapon around and blasted at the creep.

The shot severed his neck, and his head fell to the side, still attached by a flap of skin. His body twitched and shook for a moment. He actually tried to stand, then fell down. He looked like something out of a zombie movie. Max pumped another two shots into his chest, and the thug went limp.

The air was thick with smoke. The couch was still on fire, burning a furious rage. Thick smoke billowed up to the ceiling, and the fire alarm sounded. Sprinklers activated, dousing the lobby with water. It was like a contained thunderstorm. Emergency fire bots rushed to extinguish the blaze.

The lobby was lined with bodies. Blood stained the bulkheads and the deck. The crimson mess was becoming diluted with each drop from the sprinklers.

The employees behind the counter cautiously peered over the ledge. The once luxurious lobby was now in ruins. The chandelier was a priceless antique from the 19th century. The marble columns had been imported from an ancient temple on Beta Altair. But the soothing music of Mozart still resonated from the robot orchestra.

Max took a deep breath. Her eyes found Winston and she smiled. But as soon as she stepped from behind the pillar, a plasma bolt rocketed through the air. The searing pain was unbearable as it ripped through her chest. It was like somebody had stuck a hot poker into her rib cage, then twisted it around, making sure they hit every internal organ. Even with her advanced pain management techniques, it hurt like a mother fucker.

The impact knocked Max off her feet. She slammed to the deck, and what little air she had left her lungs was forced out. She gasped for breath. One of the fallen goons on the ground had managed to squeeze the trigger, sending the deadly bolt into Max's chest. She mustered her last bit of strength and used it to lift her weapon and fire at the bastard who had killed her.

Max ended him in a blazing fury. Her arm dropped down to the deck after she finished the task. She desperately sucked air into her lungs, and clutched the burning hole in her chest. There was little blood. The heat had cauterized the wound, otherwise she would have bled out by now.

Winston rushed to her and knelt down to attend to her.

"I don't suppose you're programed with any medical knowledge, are you?" Max could barely choke out the words. She knew she was dying. But this time, she didn't think she was going to be revived.

31

Winston scooped Max off the floor and cradled her in his arms. He raced out of the lobby, stepping over the fallen bodies. He pushed into the corridor and raced through the crowded passageways, weaving in and out.

"Where are you taking me?" Max stammered. Her eyes were droopy, and she drifted on the brink of consciousness.

"You need immediate medical attention."

"You can't bring me to the med center. I'll be arrested by the OPD, and we don't know who we can trust—*if* we can trust anybody in that department."

"Without medical attention, you'll die."

"No hospitals!"

Winston said nothing.

"No hospitals! Promise me!"

"It is against my programing to allow a human to be harmed. Not taking you to a hospital would violate that basic programming."

"There has to be another alternative," Max said.

Winston processed the situation. "I may know someone who might be able to help."

THE OPERATING ROOM didn't look clean. A layer of dust covered the antiquated equipment. Grime coated the walls and deck. Dried spots of crimson blood stained the deck by the operating table. One of the lights flickered, possibly indicating some type of short in the power supply. This didn't inspire confidence, but Max didn't have much choice. It was either this, or die.

Winston laid her down on the operating table. Doctor Matsuda ambled into the room and brushed the robot aside, grumbling for Winston to get out of the way. A cigarette dangled from his mouth, and he held a half-empty glass of scotch in his hand. Matsuda wore glasses and had long white hair. He reached up and grabbed an articulated arm that hung from the ceiling. He brought it down and hovered it over Max's body. Then he ran the scanning wand over Max's torso.

Max's eyes narrowed at the doctor, and she managed to scowl at Winston.

"Doctor Matsuda was one of the finest surgeons in the city," Winston said in an upbeat, optimistic voice.

"Was?" Max muttered.

"Lost my license," Matsuda said. He flashed a disarming smile.

Max's eyes widened, and she fidgeted on the table, trying to sit up.

"Be still," Matsuda said. "You'll blur the scan."

Max reclined and tried to relax.

Matsuda finished passing the wand over her body,

and a detailed 3D image of her internal organs appeared on a display screen. Matsuda was able to manipulate the scan data and look at the injuries from every conceivable angle. The medical AI ran a diagnostic. A few moments later, the computer displayed a detailed report of all the suspected injuries.

Matsuda squinted as he looked at the display. He puffed on his cigarette, and the cherry glowed orange. He pulled the cigarette from his lips and flicked the ashes onto the deck, then stuck it back between his lips where it dangled once again.

Max wondered if he was going to continue smoking during the operation.

"You're in bad shape," Matsuda said.

"Thanks, Einstein. Can you fix me?"

Matsuda shrugged.

"How did you lose your license?" Her speech was labored and difficult.

"Wrongful death."

A look of terror washed over Max's face. She looked even more pale and sickly than before. Sweat beaded on her forehead. Matsuda grabbed an injection gun and loaded it with a vial of medication. He placed the nozzle against Max's arm.

"What is that?"

"Light sedative." He squeezed the trigger, and the vial of clear liquid emptied. Max felt the warm sensation wash over her body, starting at the injection site. Her pulse and respiration slowed. A wave of soothing calm enveloped her. A slight smile curled on her lips. She no longer cared about anything. Her surroundings became a tad blurry. As she glanced around the operating room, she noticed posters of animal anatomy—

dogs, cats, Flotrixian morfgs. When she spoke, her words were slightly slurred. "Are you a fucking veterinarian?"

"One of the finest in the city," Winston interjected.

Max rolled her eyes.

Matsuda took a pair of scissors and cut away the fabric surrounding the wound. The process exposed a little bit of her breast.

"Watch it there…"

"I'm a medical professional. I've seen it all before."

"You *were* a medical professional," Max snarked.

"Do you want to be awake, or asleep, for the procedure?" Matsuda asked.

"Awake. I'm definitely keeping an eye on you."

Matsuda nodded in agreement. He injected her with an anesthetic, which promptly knocked her out. "She talks too much. Ruins my concentration."

Matsuda pressed a button on the RISS (Robotic Intelligence Surgical System) machine. Multiple arms swung down from the ceiling, each with specialized instruments. The surgical system moved with speed and precision, debriding the necrotic tissue, re-vascularizing damaged structures, and repairing the trauma.

Matsuda leaned back and relaxed, taking a drag from his cigarette and sipping the scotch. That was the extent of his job now. The machine would diagnose and treat the patient. Modern doctors were essentially computer techs—making sure the machines ran smoothly, overseeing their diagnostic evaluations and proposed surgical solutions. 99% of the time, the RISS system was flawless. But a virus, corrupted file, or fluctuation in power could result in catastrophic outcomes.

In the old days, the surgery would have taken

several hours. But the estimated time of repair for the robotic system was less than 20 minutes. Matsuda poured another drink and lit another cigarette. By the time he finished those two indulgences, the automated surgeon would be closing the wound—if all went well.

Matsuda stepped to the control terminal and monitored Max's vitals. The computer displayed a list of actions taken during the surgery and also displayed a confidence interval of probable success. A trained monkey could do Matsuda's job, at least until things went wrong. The sudden flickering on the display screen was an indication that something wasn't right. A moment later, the computer crashed. The robotic arms, once operating the precise ballet of surgery, froze in their tracks. The overhead lights flickered out, and Matsuda found himself enveloped in darkness.

This was not good.

If Matsuda didn't get the power back and the system online, Max would be a goner.

32

Matsuda frantically tried to get the system to reboot. But the power was out throughout the med center. The only light in the room was coming from the glow behind Winston's eyes and various points on his body.

Winston activated emergency floodlights positioned in his brow. "What's wrong?"

"Power fluctuation. The grid is unstable."

"Does this happen often?"

Matsuda shrugged. "Occasionally. Come with me."

Winston followed Matsuta as he raced out of the operating room. Winston's lights illuminated the corridor as the doctor made his way to a storage compartment. The hatch wouldn't slide open because of the power outage. Matsuda manually released the locking mechanism, and he and Winston slid the hatch aside. Matsuda dashed inside, still puffing on his cigarette. The amber glow illuminated his face as Winston tried to light the compartment from behind him.

"Probably tripped a breaker. The power grid in this section of the station leaves a lot to be desired." Matsuda opened the breaker box and flipped several switches, but the power didn't come back on. He tried again without success.

"Don't you have a backup power system for the OR?" Winston asked.

"I did. But it broke."

"Redundant power systems are required by law in critical medical facilities."

"Do you know how expensive those things are to fix?"

"I'm not exactly getting rich over here removing kidney stones from cats."

"We can use my power system. I can shut down my functions to minimize the draw. That should be enough to operate RISS device."

"Matsuda nodded.

The two raced back into the operating room, and Matsuda connected the surgical terminal to Winston's power port. It was located behind the body panel in his abdomen. It functioned as a two-way charge station. Winston powered himself down. He knew there was a possibility this would be the last time he attained consciousness. The surgical system was a heavy draw—it would deplete his battery quickly. There's also the possibility that it would overload his circuitry. Winston may not have technically been alive, but he sure didn't want to cease to exist. His programming didn't allow him to let a human being be harmed, and by not utilizing his power supply he would have been complicit in Max's demise. But even without the programming, Winston probably would've risked his being. It was just the kind of robot that he was.

Matsuda powered up and rebooted the surgical system. The robotic arms swung back into action. Vital signs displayed on the monitor. Everything was low— pulse, respiration, oxygen saturation, blood pressure. One of the robotic arms placed an oxygen mask over Max's nose and mouth. The surgical system injected medication to boost blood pressure and elevate the heart rate. After a few moments, Max's vital signs normalized.

Sparks flew from Winston, and smoke wafted from his body panels. The power draw was overloading his system.

The robotic arms applied a regenerative compound, then sealed Max's wound with an adhesive gel. It formed a perfect skin seal. The robotic arms retracted to their resting position—their portion of the surgery complete.

Matsuda studied the readout on the display termi-nal. Despite the interruption, the system was predicting a 96% chance of success.

The lights flickered on as main power was restored to the operating room. Matsuda disconnected Winston from the power cable and plugged it back into its normal socket. He continued to monitor Max's vital signs, making sure they were all within the range of normal. When he was sure she was stable, he turned his attention to Winston.

Matsuda waved his hand, fanning the smoke away from the robot. It was hard to say just how much damage had been done. Matsuda was familiar with troubleshooting robotic equipment, and dealing with

robots like Winston was far less complicated than troubleshooting the surgical system.

Matsuda tried to initiate a reboot of Winston's
system, but the android was non-responsive. Matsuda
hoisted Winston up and carried him to a gurney. He set
the robot down and began to remove the body panels.
He surveyed Winston's internal structures for damage.
Matsuda hooked a cable into one of Winston's I/O ports
and connected him to the computer. The diagnostic scan
returned several faults within Winston's circuitry. One
of the printed circuit boards had been completely fried.
The lead wires from the battery pack had melted, and
the remaining charge was suspect. The power cells had
been damaged and would likely never return to their
full capacity.

If Matsuda was able to get Winston functioning
again, and that was a big *if,* there was no telling how
long his power supply would last. The robot would
need a thorough reconditioning.

33

M ax stirred as the anesthesia wore off. Her droopy eyes peeled open, and she struggled to focus. For a moment, she had almost forgotten where she was, or what had happened.

Doctor Matsuda hovered over her, another cigarette dangling from his lips.

Max's vision finally sharpened. She made the mistake of attempting to sit up, which caused a sharp pain to stab through her chest, tugging at the newly sealed skin. It felt like someone had stuck a kitchen knife through her flesh. She winced and laid her head back down, and the discomfort subsided.

"Rest—good. Activity—bad," Matsuda said.

Max glanced around the room looking for Winston. "Where's the robot?"

"He's toast."

"What do you mean?"

"We had a slight malfunction during the operation," Matsuda stammered. "Winston served as a backup battery. He sacrificed himself to save you."

Max's heart sank. Winston was beginning to grow on her. She couldn't help but feel touched by his sacrifice. "Is he salvageable?"

Matsuda shrugged. "We'll see."

"What about his data center? He contains valuable information."

"If I can activate his neural processor, then I can better understand the extent of the damage. The diagnostic scan shows no damage to his storage device, but you never really know."

Max grimaced as she forced herself to sit up, using her hands to push herself from the table. Her chest was on fire.

"You need to rest. Take time to heal."

"I don't have time to heal," Max grumbled.

"Don't blame me if you rupture something and bleed to death internally."

Max scowled at him and eased herself off the operating table.

Matsuda rushed to assist her. "You shouldn't be up and walking around. You've undergone major surgery, and you are pumped full of drugs. You're not going to be steady on your feet for several hours."

"I process medication fast," she said, still slightly slurring her words. Max glanced down at the gaping hole in her fitted top. The wound had been sprayed with a protective synthetic skin. It was roughly the same color as normal flesh, but slightly translucent. The hole in her top exposed a significant portion of flesh, along with a healthy dose of side-boob. "My tit is going to flop right out of this thing."

"Sorry, I'm all out of fitted bodysuits," Matsuda said dryly.

"Hand me that role of surgical tape," Max said, pointing to a nearby instrument cart.

Matsuda complied. Max used the tape to secure the fabric around the affected area. It looked a little funny, but it would prevent a nipple malfunction. And it sure was better than wearing one of those ugly green hospital gowns. Though she figured Matsuda didn't have any of those around that would fit her, seeing how most of his clients were small animals. She got a mental image in her head of a dachshund wearing a hospital gown, and the thought gave her a slight chuckle. But the chuckle made her cringe with pain.

"Try not to laugh," Matsuda said. He helped her hobble over to Winston. Max felt like a decrepit old lady.

"You have another circuit board?" Max asked as her sad eyes surveyed Winston's disabled remains.

"Let me see what I can dig up." Matsuda rummaged through drawers, but came up empty-handed. He stepped out of the operating room and returned a few moments later with a circuit board pilfered from a broken maintenance bot.

"Do you think that's going to work?"

"Only one way to find out," Matsuda said. "His neural processing core seems to be intact and undamaged. It's the power regulating chip that got fried, which is a pretty standard part."

Matsuda replaced the circuit board, and rewired the battery connections. Once he reattached the body panels, he powered Winston on. The robot's eyes came alive, and his appendages flexed, like an involuntary response. Winston stared like a zombie into space for a moment until his boot sequence completed. His eyes flicked from Matsuda to Max. "I see that the surgery was successful. I am relieved. I was worried about you."

Max smiled at him. "I was worried about you too."

"How many fingers am I holding up?" Matsuda asked.

"Two," Winston replied, correctly.

"Hold out both of your arms."

Winston did as he asked.

"Open and close your hands."

Winston's mechanical fingers extended and contracted. He appeared to be functioning properly.

Matsuda handed him a glass beaker.

Winston clasped it without shattering the glass. "My self diagnostics indicate that I am operating at full capacity—although my power management system is operating inefficiently, and my response time is slower than normal. Perhaps due to replaced circuit board. It's an older model. I'm also detecting irregularities in my power supply. Other than that, I'm fine."

"Is your memory intact?" Max asked. "Do you still have all of the incriminating data against Thornton?"

34

Winston searched his data storage device with a worried look on his face. "I have full access to my short and long-term memory. But I cannot seem to access my data storage. I'm sorry, but the data appears to be lost."

Max frowned.

"I know this is a major disappointment to you." Max forced a smile. "No. The important thing is that you're alive."

"As I've said before, I am not actually alive."

"You know what I mean." Max pondered the situation. Without any hard evidence, Thornton was going to get away with his weapons trafficking. Weapons of mass destruction would fall into the hands of terrorists, and countless innocent civilians could die. But Max wasn't about to let any of that happen. "Maybe the data is corrupted? Perhaps you just can't access it?" Max was hopeful.

Winston shrugged.

Max pulled her mobile from her pocket and called Dylan—a strange woman answered.

"I'm looking for Dylan," Max said. "Who is this?"

"It doesn't matter who this is. If you ever want to see Dylan alive again, you'll bring us the robot. You've got an hour to comply. If you've made copies of the robot's data, Dylan dies."

"What if I just take the robot straight to the FCIS?" Max was bluffing.

"You don't want to do that."

"Why not? You, and your boss, and everyone else involved in this little scheme is going to go down."

"Go ahead, do that—your boyfriend dies."

"Whoever said he was my boyfriend?"

There was a long pause on the other end of the line. "I doubt you're going to let an innocent person go to the grave over a robot."

"You clearly don't know the first thing about me," Max said. "If you did, you wouldn't be threatening me. I'm the last person in the galaxy that you want to piss off. I mean, how many people did you send after me? At least a dozen? And what happened to them? Oh, yeah, that's right... they're all dead now. So why don't you tell your boss that I'm coming for him. And if you ass-clowns hurt Dylan, I'm not just going to kill you, I'm going to make sure each and every last one of you knows the meaning of suffering."

There was a long pause. "Are you done talking tough?" the woman said. "Now it's my turn. Bring the robot to docking Bay 72. Come alone." The woman chuckled. "You Ultra punks always were full of yourselves."

"You're the shooter. You killed Chace."

Max could almost hear the woman grin. There was a silent acknowledgment.

"I'm looking forward to meeting you, face-to-face," the woman said. She ended the call.

Max didn't know who this woman was, or how she knew about project SW Ultra. She was probably some type of special forces. Max would find out soon enough.

"There's no harm in turning me over," Winston said. "Without my data, I am useless."

"Yeah, but they don't know that," Max said. "And I'm not handing you over to anybody."

"What are you planning on doing?" Winston asked.

"Just what I said I was going to do. They want a fight, they're going to get it."

"You are in no condition," Matsuda said.

"Where's my pistol?"

Matsuda gave her a look like she was crazy. He shook his head and ambled to a drawer, pulling out her holster and Bösch-Hauer RK-229 pistol, as well as the Krüger-Schmitt P-385 pistol she had taken from the goon in the hotel suite. The Bösch-Hauer was empty, and the magazine for the Krüger-Schmitt was less than half-full.

Max strapped the holster around her waist, checked over the P-385, and holstered it. The 229 wasn't going to do her any good. She could set the 229's plasma generator to overload and use the weapon as a time delayed grenade. But she wasn't exactly going into this thing with an awesome array of firepower. Outnumbered, outgunned, and in a weakened physical condition—in Max's mind, that was a level playing field.

Doctor Matsuda took a deep breath. He had a look on his face like he was about to do something he shouldn't. He ambled over to a medicine cabinet, grabbed a few vials and the injection gun, and strolled back to Max. He held up one of the vials and loaded it into the injector. "This is a local anesthetic. I can numb the area to the point you won't feel a thing. It should last a few hours."

Max gave him a nod of approval, and Matsuda injected the anesthetic directly into the affected area. The initial shot stung like hell, but soon, her entire thoracic cavity grew numb.

Matsuda held up another vile. "This one is a neuro-stimulant. You'll have more energy, quicker reaction times, and enhanced endurance. But the crash is severe."

"How long will it last?"

"An hour. Maybe two?"

"And what's the crash like?"

"Brain fog, lethargy, poor neuromuscular coordina-tion. You'll be worthless."

"Well, I better get this over with quick, then."

Matsuda injected Max. A warm tingling sensation flowed through her body. It ran down her arms and legs and extended to the tips of her fingers and toes. Max already had enhanced reflexes, superior strength and endurance, and increased visual acuity—but this drug was insane. It gave her laser-like focus. It was like somebody had turned up the detail on every aspect of life. She could read the serial number on a piece of equipment from across the room. It was like she had mainlined a pot of coffee. But this was all going to come at a price.

"I got something else you might find useful," Matsuda said.

35

Max slammed the magazine into the chamber, then pulled the slide back, loading the antique weapon. It was an old Bösch-Hauer .45mm pistol. It had been Matsuda's father's sidearm during the Second Galactic War. The good doctor had fired it a few times at the range since inheriting the weapon, and he had kept it in meticulous condition. It was clean and well oiled, and the ammunition was fresh. Matsuda liked to keep the weapon handy in case any of his clients got out of hand—he didn't strictly make a living treating dogs and cats. On Orion Station, there was a large underground market for medical care among organized crime types. They couldn't exactly walk into a legitimate med center with a plasma wound without getting asked a ton of unwanted questions.

It wasn't a plasma pistol, but a .45 caliber handgun still packed a hell of a punch. And Max was happy to have received it from Matsuda. This particular model held 17 in the magazine, and one in the pipe. Max had two extra magazines. That was potentially 52 bad guys she could take out.

Max had snaked her way through a cramped air duct that led to docking Bay 72. It was a cavernous space with a flight deck large enough to accommodate a medium-sized transport. It was several stories high, and the length of a football field. An electromagnetically shielded portal remained open to space, offering an up close and personal view of the cosmos. Cargo containers and storage crates were stacked atop one another, forming dozens of rows. Several of Thornton's goons were stationed at various positions throughout the compartment. A small dropship was on the flight deck. It looked prepped and ready to go, in case of emergency.

The space was dimly lit. Work crews had long clocked out for the day, and the high-powered stadium lights were off. Instead, the area was lit by smaller sconces affixed to the bulkheads. They didn't have a lot of throw and left the majority of the bay in darkness. Aisles in between the crates and containers were bathed in shadow—plenty of space to move about undetected.

With eyes like a hawk, Max could see Thornton standing by the dropship, along with Dylan, who was bound and gagged. Max was going to have to get through a dozen goons to get to Dylan.

Winston was behind her in the shaft.

Max holstered the .45 pistol. Then she pried open the vent to the air shaft, careful not to make a sound and give away her position. Once she had removed the vent from its attachments, she pulled it back into the shaft and set it aside. She inched her head out of the passageway. She was two stories above the deck. She reached out and grabbed a maintenance rung affixed to the bulkhead, and pulled herself out of the narrow shaft. "Try not to make too much noise," she whispered to Winston.

"I won't make a sound."

Max dangled above the deck, and used the rungs to lower herself down without making a sound.

Max crept through the shadows like a phantom. The light from one of the bulkhead sconces glimmered off the razor-sharp blade of the surgical scalpel she had taken from Matsuda's operating room. It was a tool that had been used countless times to save lives. Now, Max was going to use it to take them.

She crept up behind one of the goons as he guarded the area with a plasma rifle. In a flash, the palm of Max's hand wrapped around his mouth, while the blade pressed against his neck. A quick slice opened his flesh, and rivers of blood poured from his carotid arteries. Max kept any sound from escaping his lips as his knees buckled and he crumpled to the ground. He gurgled slightly, then the last breath slipped from his lungs. A pool of blood oozed onto the deck, surrounding his carcass.

Max reached down and grabbed his plasma rifle and slung the strap over her shoulder. She slipped back into the shadows and slid between two massive crates. She waited for a guard to stroll past and eased into the aisle behind him. She tiptoed through the darkness, like a cat stalking its prey. Another glimmer of light flickered across the razor-sharp blade. Crimson blood flowed as Max severed arteries. Another goon went down.

But another guard saw her.

A flurry of plasma bolts streaked in her direction.

Max ducked for cover behind one of the containers and returned fire. The goon's head exploded, slathering a container with gooey chunks of charred flesh.

So much for the element of surprise.

Thornton's men converged on Max's position. More plasma bolts blazed at her from across a clearing. Max ducked behind a crate for cover. Sparks showered as the projectiles impacted the crate, leaving charred, smoldering pits. Wisps of smoke wafted into the air. Max angled the barrel of her newly acquired plasma rifle around the corner of the crate and unleashed a torrent of weapons fire. The gleaming projectiles raced across the compartment, incinerating an attacker.

Two more scurried down the aisle across from her. A chaotic flurry of plasma bolts erupted. Sizzling beams blazed inches away from Max. She lined the creeps up in the reticle of her sights and squeezed the trigger. Two more bodies hit the deck.

Max—5, bad guys—0.

A goon atop one of the containers blasted at her.

Max angled her weapon up and fired two shots, piercing the man's chest. He tumbled forward and cracked the deck, snapping his neck on impact.

Another attacker rounded the corner at the end of the aisle and opened fire.

Max tumbled to the ground, rolling to avoid the blistering projectiles whizzing all around her. She rolled onto her knee and brought the weapon into the firing position. With the quick squeeze of the trigger, several bolts raced down the aisle, dropping the assailant to the ground.

More plasma bolts rocketed at her from behind.

They lit up the containers around her, showering sparks.

Max spun around 180° and squeezed off several rounds, then slipped in between the containers, taking cover. Glowing plasma bolts blazed down the aisle. She angled her weapon around the container and squeezed off a few more rounds. Several more plasma bolts peppered the container she was hiding behind. She ducked back, avoiding the blasts.

Max edged around the corner and lined the creep up in her sights. A scorching exchange of weapons fire filled the aisle with chaos. A plasma bolt slammed into the barrel of Max's weapon, shredding it to pieces. The remains clattered to the deck in a twisted heap of smoldering debris. Blistering shrapnel tore into her hand and face.

Goddamnit! The old scars were just starting to heal, Max thought.

36

Max's flesh crackled and popped from the heat, like a steak on the grill. Wisps of smoke wafted from her flesh—a shard of scalding metal embedded into the fleshy pad between her thumb and forefinger. The pain radiated up her arm. Another piece had punctured her cheek, and she could feel the tip of it scratching against the enamel of her molars.

The first rule of shrapnel wounds is to leave them in place until you can get to a proper medical facility. Sometimes the embedded object is the only thing keeping you alive. But, for the most part, the heat tends to cauterize the wound and prevent excessive bleeding. Right now, Max just wanted these blistering pieces of metal out of her skin. But that was going to have to wait. It was time for a little payback.

Max unholstered the .45 caliber pistol and angled the barrel around the corner of the container. She hadn't fired a weapon's like this in a long time. She waited for the thug to pop his head around the corner, then lined him up in her sights. Her finger squeezed the trigger. It was a heavier draw than a standard plasma pistol, or rifle. The hammer slammed down, capping off a round. Muzzle flash lit up her face. Smoke wafted from the end of the barrel as the old-fashioned copper round rocketed down the aisle. The thunderous boom echoed off the bulkheads, and the recoil kicked the weapon back, angling her arm up a few degrees. The blast was so loud, her ears instantly rang. The energy of the weapon filled her entire body. It felt good to squeeze the trigger. It felt even better to watch the goon's head splatter, leaving a crimson mist hanging in the air. His body flopped to the deck, and pinkish-grey chunks of his brain dripped down a nearby container.

Max liked this weapon. She liked it a lot.

She used her shirtsleeve as a pad to grasp the stinging shrapnel and yank it from her hand. Her jaw clenched as the pain shot up her arm. Then she pulled the other piece from her cheek. The bloody fragments of metal clattered as she tossed them on the deck.

Max climbed up a stack of cargo containers to get a better view of the area. It hurt like hell to grip anything with her hand, but she muscled through it, shoving the pain into the far corner of her mind. She much preferred to fight from the high ground.

Several thugs approached from various rows, showering steady streams of plasma bolts in her direction. She crouched low as the plasma bolts zipped overhead. The elevation made her a difficult target, with the rim of the container offering a degree of protection.

She angled over the edge and squeezed the trigger.

BAM!

BAM!

BAM!

Another deafening cacophony of sound emanated from the weapon. Another one of Thornton's men lay flat on the deck, oozing blood from a fatal gunshot wound. His chest turned into ground hamburger meat by the hollow-point copper bullet.

Max rolled to the other side of the container and took aim at another goon that was approaching up the aisle. Max squeezed off another several rounds. The sharp smell of gunpowder filled her nose. The ringing in her ears grew louder. Shell casings pinged off the deck below. The bullets peppered the assailant, stopping his forward progression. This weapon definitely had old-school charm. She could see why some special forces units preferred them to plasma weapons. The only drawback was that she was less accurate on the second and third shots when fired in quick succession due to the recoil of the pistol.

The weapon had a big unmistakable bang that struck fear into the hearts of the enemy. There was something raw and primitive about it. She felt like a predator in the jungle, stalking its prey.

Another flurry of plasma bolts streamed past her.

Max angled her weapon around and took aim at her new attacker. She blasted off another double tap—the slide locked forward on the weapon—the magazine empty.

It didn't matter much. Her attacker was writhing on the deck with a sucking chest wound. He suffocated in a matter of moments, drowning in his own blood that was gurgling in his throat.

Max pressed the mag release button, dropped the magazine out, and smacked in another one. She pulled the slide back, loading another round into the chamber. 17 round magazines were a little limiting. They were a far cry from the higher capacity magazines of plasma rifles. The weapon definitely had logistical shortcomings, but so far it hadn't been much of an issue. Perhaps the novelty would wear off after a while.

Max cautiously climbed to her feet, scanning the area. Bodies lay strewn about, and a disconcerting quiet filled the chamber. There were no more blazing beams of plasma. No more goons were coming. Had she taken them all out?

She scanned the compartment, looking for Thornton and Dylan, but from this angle it was hard to see. And her enhanced vision seemed to be dulling. Her muscles went weak, and her energy level plummeted. Her head throbbed, and her pulse pounded in her ears. It was some kind of wicked crazy hangover. Max couldn't figure out what was happening, then she remembered Matsuda's admonition—the injection he had given her was wearing off.

Suddenly, an adversary dropped down from a catwalk. The figure slammed on top of the container like a superhero plummeting off a tall building. Max spun her weapon around to take out the intruder. But her reflexes were slow, like in a bad dream. The mysterious figure kicked the weapon out of Max's hands. The gunmetal gray pistol clattered across the deck, discharging upon impact.

Before Max could react, the business end of a plasma pistol stared her in the face. It belonged to an athletic woman with dark hair, and a similar build to Max. It had to be the woman she talked to earlier. It had to be the person that killed Chace Carter. But who the hell was she?

37

"**Y**ou're not a former *Reaper*," Max said, surveying her adversary. "Not enough honor."

The woman sneered at her.

"You're not *X-force*." Max's eyes narrowed. "You're Cobra Company."

"You're smarter than you look," the woman said.

Cobra Company supplied the Federation with special operators on an independent contractor basis. Word around the cosmos had it they were trying to create their own perfect super-soldier. Maybe they had done it? They'd sell their services to the highest bidder. This woman was clearly a hired gun, working for Thornton.

"We haven't been properly introduced," the woman said. "I'm Clarissa... and you're dead."

She was about to squeeze the trigger when a plasma blast hit the pistol, knocking it from her hand. She recoiled, and her head snapped toward the origin of the blast.

Winston crouched in the air shaft. He had fired a shot with pinpoint accuracy at the barrel of Clarissa's weapon. Technically, he was complying with his primary coding. He was protecting human life, and wasn't harming anyone by firing at the weapon.

Max sprung to her feet, spinning a roundhouse kick that connected with Clarissa's jaw. The impact snapped Clarissa's neck to the side and drew blood from her lip. But it didn't seem to faze her. She turned her head back to Max, and a slight grin curled on her lips. "I hope you've got more than that."

Max would normally wipe the floor with this wannabe, but in her sluggish state she was less than her usual self. Max swung a hard right, but it felt like she was punching underwater. She couldn't move fast enough.

Clarissa dodged, and blocked the punch with ease. She countered with a left hook that connected with Max's jaw, sending her crashing down. Clarissa put her foot into Max's rib cage. Pain stabbed through her thoracic cavity. Clarissa had kicked Max directly on her surgical site.

Max flopped over, crashing against the container top. She mustered all of her strength and attempted to stagger to her feet, but Clarissa mashed another swift kick into Max's jaw. The force snapped her head back, and she rolled off the edge of the container, dropping several stories to the deck.

The impact knocked all the air out of Max's lungs. She gasped for breath, desperately trying to suck oxygen into her lungs. But it seemed like they wouldn't fill.

Clarissa climbed down to finish the job.

Max was huddling on all fours, attempting to stand. She finally made it to her feet, swaying like a drunk.

Clarissa could taste victory. Max could see it in her eyes—the woman had a sadistic grin. She walked Max down, pushing closer. She jabbed twice, then swung another right. The blow stunned Max, but she managed to stay on her feet. Clarissa caught her with a left uppercut. The blow rattled Max's teeth and sent her crashing back down.

"This is too easy. You are starting to bore me."

Max tongued a row of teeth, trying to feel for a chipped tooth, but they all seemed to remain intact.

Clarissa glanced around and saw the body of a fallen comrade. She eyed the plasma rifle lying on the deck by the corpse. She strolled for the weapon.

It was now or never for Max. She had to shake off whatever was dragging her down. Her advanced genetics had allowed her to process the neuro-stimulant faster than normal. She hoped it would allow her to bounce back just as quickly. Max summoned all her strength and sprang to her feet. She charged at Clarissa, attempting to tackle her before she reached the plasma rifle. She ran as fast as she could. She felt lethargic at first. But failure was not acceptable. Defeat was not an option. She let out a primal scream and muscled through the sluggishness. She careened toward Clarissa, wrapping her up like a defensive linebacker, slamming her to the deck. Max did the old *ground and pound*, unleashing a hailstorm of fists.

Left.

Right.

Left.

Right.

Each one connecting with Clarissa's face. The slap of fists against flesh echoed off the containers. The crunching sound of knuckles against bone filled Max's ears. It was a beautiful sound.

But Clarissa managed to throw Max off her. She tumbled away as Clarissa scurried toward the weapon. Her fingertips found the rifle stock, and Clarissa pulled the weapon toward her.

Max grabbed Clarissa by the ankle and yanked her away from the rifle.

Clarissa's fingertips clawed against the deck as she was dragged away from the prize. Now it was Max's turn to put a boot into Clarissa's rib cage.

Ribs snapped.

Max kicked her again with everything she had. Clarissa flopped aside and Max started for the rifle. She snatched it from the deck and brought it into the firing position. Before Clarissa could react, Max fired two plasma bolts—one into her chest, one into her head.

Carissa's body crumpled to the deck, smoke wafting from the plasma holes. Her flesh sizzled for a few moments.

Max scoffed and muttered snidely, "Cobra Company." She shook her head, then headed for Thornton. But he had realized it was time to vacate the premises.

Thornton was dragging Dylan toward the dropship with a plasma pistol to his head. Thornton stopped Max before she got too close. "Don't come any closer, or he dies."

38

Thornton used Dylan as cover. The only available target was Thornton's head, and his hand as he pressed the barrel against Dylan's temple.

Max attempted to align the reticle of her sights on Thornton's right eye. But her vision still wasn't 100%, and her hands shook with a slight tremor, still suffering the effects from coming off of the neuro-stimulant.

Max hesitated for a moment, unsure. She wanted to blow this creep's head off, but a slight miscalculation could vaporize Dylan instead.

Max's heartbeat elevated, and a rare streak of indecision befuddled her mind. Max was used to clear and concise action. No hesitation. She executed plans of attack with swift and decisive force. Technical precision. But now she found herself worrying about the outcome. Worrying about Dylan. Second-guessing her own abilities. It could be a fatal combination.

Max knew that more than half the game was in the mind. The moment you let the possibility of failure creep into the dark recesses of your brain, the more likely you are to fail.

Max's hesitation cost her. Before she could squeeze the trigger, she felt the barrel of a plasma pistol press against the back of her skull.

"Set the weapon down," a female voice behind her said.

Max recognized the voice—it was Officer Calhoun.

"Drop the weapon, now!"

Max tossed her plasma rifle to the deck. She knew her death would follow momentarily. She needed to stall for time, and she needed to get a clear view of Officer Calhoun's positioning. Max slowly turned her head to the side, trying to get a glimpse over her shoulder of Calhoun from the corner of her eye. "Is Thornton paying you *that* much?"

"Yes, actually," Calhoun said. "But it's not about the money. It's more than that."

"I don't know why I didn't see it before," Max muttered to herself. "It was plain as day." She was putting the pieces together. Max was mad at herself for not seeing through Calhoun from the start. "You had me fooled. I genuinely thought you cared about Chace."

"He showed up sniffing around," Calhoun said. "It didn't take long to make him for a Federation agent. I got close to him to find out what he was up to. I don't expect you to understand. But what we're doing here is important."

Max scoffed. "Important? Supplying terrorists with doomsday weapons? That's important?"

"The Federation is a cesspool of corruption. Their oppressive policies and colonialist actions must be stopped. They impose their worldview and culture on the galaxy without a second thought."

"Somehow I think your boss is just in this for the money," Max said. "Countless millions of people will die because of your actions. The Federation provides peace and security for the colonies."

"You're blinded by your patriotism. You need to open your eyes"

"My eyes are open," Max said. With a fluid motion, Max ducked her head and shifted to the side. She rotated towards Calhoun, swinging her left arm underneath Calhoun's trigger arm. Max raised her arm up, trapping Calhoun's, then slammed an elbow into the officer's throat. She followed up with a knee to Calhoun's belly. While still trapping Calhoun's arm, Max crossed her right hand over and grabbed the barrel of the plasma pistol, then twisted it backwards, snapping Calhoun's finger in the trigger guard. Even in Max's groggy state, the whole movement happened in a flash. It was an operatic masterpiece of precision and timing. Max stripped the pistol from Calhoun's hand and spun around to face Thorton, lining him up in her sights.

This time she didn't hesitate.

She squeezed the trigger, and plasma projectiles rocketed toward Thornton. His square head exploded, painting Dylan in crimson blood. Thornton's body crumbled, and his pistol clattered to the deck.

Max moved to Dylan and untied him. He gasped for breath as she removed the gag from his mouth.

"You're pretty handy with that thing," Dylan said.

"I get lucky every now and then," Max said, feigning modesty.

Dylan crouched down and grabbed Thornton's weapon, then moved to secure Officer Calhoun. She was writhing on the ground, gasping for air with a crushed windpipe.

"I'm going to have fun interrogating this one. I bet she has a plethora of useful information. That is, if she lives that long."

Calhoun looked almost blue in the face. She coughed and gasped, finally able to draw air into her lungs.

Dylan reached down and grabbed Calhoun's handcuffs from her utility belt, then he slapped them on her wrists. Dylan was going to take her back to FCIS headquarters. She was going to be brought up on multiple Federation charges.

"You know, you made a hell of a mess for me to clean up," Dylan said to Max in a lighthearted tone.

"I'm sure you'll sort it all out." Max smiled, but it was short-lived. The pain in her cheek from the shrapnel wound put an end to her grin. Blood was oozing from the surgical site on her chest, seeping through what remained of the protective skin-like cover —it had taken quite a bit of abuse during Max's siege of the bay.

Max had summoned all of her strength to push through her injuries, and the effects of the neuro-stimulant withdrawal. But now that the battle was over, and the urgency was gone, her adrenaline levels crashed. Her face went pale, and her knees wobbled. Then she crashed to the deck.

39

"I told you to be careful," Dr. Matsuda said, chastising Max.

She woke up in a in an intermediate care unit in Matsuda's surgical center. A screen displayed her vital signs—blood pressure, oxygen saturation, and the peaks and valleys of her heartbeat. She had an IV sticking into her forearm, and wireless electrodes stuck to various points on her body.

Dylan, Winston, and the doctor hovered over her as she regained consciousness. Their faces looked fuzzy for a moment as Max blinked her eyes, trying to see.

"This little adventure of yours caused massive internal hemorrhaging. I had to open you up and operate again."

Max rolled her eyes. "You mean, you pressed a button, and the robotic surgical system did all the work?"

Matsuda scowled at her. "It takes a great deal of expertise and knowledge to interpret the diagnostic scans and program in the appropriate surgery."

"Whatever. Am I going to live?"

"Until you go and do something stupid again," Matsuda said. "And, by the way, I want my pistol back."

"A .45?" Dylan asked.

Matsuda nodded.

"We collected it as evidence from Bay 72. I'll be sure to get it back to you."

"How long have I been out?" Max asked.

"Two days," Matsuda said. "But I may have to give you another sedative."

"Why?"

"Because you're doing that thing with your mouth again."

"What thing?"

"Talking."

Max scowled at Matsuda playfully.

"I, for one, am thankful that you are still alive," Winston said.

"I wouldn't be here without your sharpshooting skills," Max said.

"Well, I certainly owe you a debt of gratitude," Dylan said. "You ever thought about working for the FCIS? We could use good agents."

Max shook her head emphatically. "No. No more government jobs."

"Come on. It's not so bad. Gotta be better than picking up merc work?"

Max shook her head again.

"How about I call you every now and then for those difficult cases? On an independent contractor basis?" Dylan had a hopeful tone in his voice.

"I thought you might call me for non-work-related business," she said with a grin.

"I just might, if you're lucky."

Max arched an eyebrow at him.

"Oh, by the way, I tracked down your luggage." He held up a small bag. Max traveled extremely light. "When I mentioned it was a matter of Federation security, the space-line had it back to me in no time."

"Bonus points for you," Max said with a smile.

"Perks of the job."

Max winced as she tried to sit up.

"Whoa, take it easy there," Dylan said. "What exactly do you think you're doing?"

"I'm getting up and getting dressed."

"I think you need to take it easy for a few days."

Max chuckled, as if she could ever sit around taking it easy.

Dylan looked to Matsuda for support.

"She's stubborn. Good luck trying to get her to listen to anything. If she wants to re-injure herself, that's her business." Matsuda shook his head and walked away.

"You don't think I'm going to stick around this joint, do you?" Max said. "The corruption around here is systemic."

"I got a team of agents here. We found the Crygon Spheres and they've been shipped back to headquarters. Officer Calhoun's in custody, and I'm overseeing an official investigation. I can guarantee your safety while I'm here on Orion Station. I promise to look after you personally, if you will stay until you're fully recovered."

"I can take care of myself," she said in her adorably sassy way.

"As you've demonstrated."

"But, if you're agreeing to be my personal body-guard. Then I could be persuaded to stick around for a few days, I guess." She had a flirtatious glint in her eyes.

Dylan smiled. "Good."

"Mainly so I can spend more time with Winston," Max said, pretending not to be overly interested. "He's quite charming."

"Why, thank you, ma'am." Winston lit up with glee.

"And you," Dylan said pointing to the robot. "You're getting a full refurb, courtesy of the FCIS."

"Excellent."

"Provided you allow us to attempt to recover the data on your hard drives."

"I find that acceptable." Winston smiled, but it quickly faded. "It won't hurt, will it?"

Dylan chuckled. "Of course not."

Matsuda marched back into the compartment. "Okay, enough. Everybody out. The patient needs to rest." He motioned to Max. "Back in bed. I don't want any arguments. I will sedate you, if need be."

Max frowned and grumbled under her breath. "Yes, boss." She sighed.

Matsuda was surprised by how easily she complied.

"Can somebody bring me something to eat?" Max asked. "I'm starving."

"What do you want?" Dylan replied.

"Pizza."

Dylan glanced to Matsuda to see if it was okay. He shrugged.

"What kind?"

"Pineapple, mushroom, and onions." Max's eyes glimmered with anticipation.

"Really?"

"Really. It's good. Trust me."

Dylan shrugged. "Okay. But don't consider this a date, or anything."

"I won't." Max winked. "You're going to take me someplace fancy if we go on a date."

Dylan chuckled. "Deal."

The room cleared and Matsuda left Max alone. Her eyes grew heavy, and she wondered if Matsuda had slipped a sedative into her IV. Consciousness faded away, and she drifted back to sleep, dreaming of her next adventure—dreaming of catching up with Silas Rage and avenging Doctor Tor's death.

When Dylan returned with the pizza, he didn't have the heart to wake her. He pulled up a chair beside her bed and watched her sleep. He was smitten with her, no doubt about it. There was no one else in the galaxy quite like Max Mars.

THANK YOU!

I hope you enjoyed this story as much as I enjoyed writing it. Please consider reviewing the series on Amazon—a simple "Loved it," or, "Hated it," would be appreciated.

—Tripp

The Planetary Defense Force Wants YOU!

Join my newsletter and never miss a new release. No spam. Ever. Just cool stuff. (*All the cool kids are joining up.*)

See All of My Books!
Tripp Ellis Catalogue

THE GALACTIC WARS SERIES

THE TARVAAX WAR SERIES

Pursuit of Valor

Search for Honor

AUTHOR'S NOTE

You've made it this far, and you're still reading! Thank you! I really enjoyed writing Max Mars. I wanted to write a bad ass character that I could drop into almost any scenario. So, if you enjoyed this story, I'll keep finding more scenarios to put Max in.

For me, writing these books has been pure escapism. And I hope that Max Mars has given you a small little escape as well. Every day I get to travel to an amazing new world and dream up outlandish tales of adventure. This week, a pipe burst in my house, and I had to rip out sheetrock and carpet, and remediate the damage. It was really nice to be able to escape to Orion Station and deal with Max's problems instead of my own.

I love science fiction and thrillers, and I thought Max Mars was a perfect way to blend the two genres. I'm a sucker for a good mystery. The minute someone gets killed in a book or movie, I want to know who did it, and why. I love reading a good page turner.

Max Mars is smart, witty, sexy, and a total bad ass. Designing the cover was a lot of fun. I felt like *Gary & Wyatt* in *Weird Science* designing the perfect woman. I always design the book cover before I begin writing, so, I'm off to design the next Max Mars book cover. Thanks again for reading—writing has been a life-changing experience for me, and that's all because of you.

Wishing you the best,
Tripp

CONNECT WITH ME

I'm just a geek who loves sci-fi and horror. I was abducted by aliens and forced to travel the galaxy as the official biographer of an evil galactic ruler. This is where I learned to hone my craft. Fortunately, I escaped and made my way back to Earth, and now I write about my adventures. I hope you enjoy!

TRIPP ELLIS

www.trippellis.com

Made in the USA
San Bernardino, CA
12 August 2017